Furiousfotog

BROKEN DEEDS MC

SECOND GENERATION #9

By Esther E. Schmidt

Cover design by:

Esther E. Schmidt

Editor #1:

Christi Durbin

Editor #2:

Virginia Tesi Carey

Cover model:

Tony Brettman

Photographer:

Golden Czermak, FuriousFotog

CHAPTER ONE

ARROW

Wyatt shuts down the SUV when he's parked in front of the clubhouse. I grab my bag, get out, and swing it over my shoulder.

"Thanks again, brother," I tell my VP.

He's the one who picked me up from the airport. I've spent the past two months recovering in Ryckerdan, a large island in the Pacific Ocean. Archer is the president of Broken Deeds and his sister worked with their brother, Spence. His chapter is in New Jersey where they mainly do undercover assignments.

Their sister met–and married–the prince of Ryckerdan a few years ago and now she's the fucking queen. Need I mention the prince was a damn assignment at first? Yeah, we all love complications, more like colliding with that shit on a regular basis.

I was forced to take a break to not only recover from the gunshot wounds I suffered due to protecting...yeah, let's skip over those pesky little details and keep it nice and short; I had to recover and take a break from everything. Two months in paradise sounds great for some, but I'm man enough to say I'm glad to be back.

"Don't mention it," Wyatt rumbles.

The first person I see when I step inside the clubhouse is my half-sister, Hadley. She's downright amazing and I love her. We even work in the same club-owned tattoo shop. Since Hadley is older than me and deaf, I learned ASL right along with learning how to talk. I don't even notice her signing; my brain automatically interprets it just as fast as someone else would use his mouth to talk.

"There you are," she signs and gives me a hug. Quickly pulling back she starts to sign again. "Can I put you back on the schedule? We've missed you at the shop."

I grin down at her, drop the bag I was holding, and instead of my mouth, I use my hands to tell her, "Sure. Can't wait."

"Okay, darlin'. Let's give your brother a little space to catch his breath." Vachs has his arm around my sister's middle and has her plastered to his front while he rumbles out his words. "Welcome home, brother."

I lift my chin in silent appreciation. My sister is his old lady, has been for years. Even though the man has learned ASL, he still talks to her as if she can hear him. He knows she can't, though that doesn't stop him from doing so.

The man always makes sure some part of her is connected to his chest so I'm sure it's all about the vibrations. She loves him and he's good to her. Treats her like the treasure she is and not as someone with a disability.

Ganza steps toward me and leans in close. "Dude. You have some timing or your girl has, but what are the odds of her showing up the same day you come home? Oh, now I get it. It's not a coincidence. You arranged for her to come here, right?"

Confusion washes over me. My girl? "What are you talking about? Who showed up here?"

"Ginerva. I saw Archer taking her into his office not ten minutes before you showed up." Now he's the one sporting a confused look.

Fuck. I knew there was a chance I'd see her around town, but I didn't expect to see her so soon. Ginerva. Ginny. The woman I took bullets for. Ginny was a rookie cop and kidnapped by a human trafficking ring. I went in undercover and picked her out of a damn book with pictures when I had to pick a girl for a date.

A date. Meaning fuck her any way I'd like and if I like it hard and rough and end up killing her? No worries, the human trafficking ring would take care of the mess. All of it for the low price of fifteen thousand dollars. During the undercover mission we found out she wasn't just a woman but a rookie cop.

We needed time to get shit together if we wanted to take down everyone involved. We had to make a hard choice and it was a club decision that we let Ginny choose her fate. So, I gave her a choice when I went in for that fucked-up date. Either I'd save just her, or she'd have to go back to her kidnappers and relay information to me so basically go undercover as well. That strong woman chose to help other women instead of saving her own ass.

In the end, it almost killed her. She would have died if I didn't take those bullets for her. Fuck. I'm no damn hero. Not by a long shot, but in my book I owed her. Still owe her for what we did together. For what I did…what she asked for us to do. I swallow hard and shove my guilty conscience for giving her what she asked for–and fucking loved doing it–back into the dark hole where it needs to stay.

Not explaining anything to anyone, I stomp into the direction of Archer's office and rasp my knuckles against the door.

"Yeah?" my prez bellows from inside.

I enter his office and completely ignore the entire room and everything in it; focusing solely on the man behind the desk.

The coward that I am completely ignores Ginny when I ask my Prez, "Why is she here?"

"Because no one will believe me," Ginny snaps. "But I realize coming here was a mistake as well."

This time I risk a glance her way and I instantly regret doing so. Fucking hell. She cut her hair. All of it is gone and instead of the sea of light color she had two months ago, it's now dark blue and a pixie cut. Shit. Probably due to her captivity where they dragged her by the hair if they needed her to move.

Archer sighs. "It's not a mistake, Ginerva. The things you've brought to my attention will be checked."

"Checked." She snorts. "Right. Sounds like the exact same thing my chief said when I told him the biker isn't part of an official motorcycle club but is a cop instead." Her voice turns into a mocking, baritone one when she adds, "I'll look into it, dear. Why don't you take a few more weeks of paid leave and be sure to get the psychological evaluation. Then we will discuss your options." Her warm, honey-colored eyes turn cold when she snaps, "I'm not crazy.

I know who I saw and heard."

The fuck? The biker she mentioned is probably the one who requested her to be kidnapped. I have no damn clue what she's been through but the "date" we had turned out to be recorded. They wanted to blackmail me in case they needed help handling the motorcycle club which they also did business with. Now she's saying it wasn't a biker but a fucking cop?

"No one is disagreeing with you or saying you're crazy, Ginerva," Archer calmly states. "But you know damn well the psychological evaluation is mandatory."

Ginny swallows hard and I can tell by the way her hands clench and unclench she's trying damn hard to hold it together.

She gives my prez a tight nod. "Thank you for listening." Her voice is firm and final as she spins around to head for the door.

"Ginerva," Archer grunts and waits till she connects her gaze with his before he adds, "Don't go digging into this by yourself. You've done enough already, and if you say this biker is a cop? He will find out there's a witness out there to point him out. Revenge blinds you. Understand what I'm saying."

"Thanks for bringing it to my attention," she mockingly states and mutters under her breath, "So much for her suggestion to ask Broken Deeds for help."

"Motherfucker," Archer grumbles under his breath, but it's her last words that snag my attention.

I reach out and wrap my hand around her upper arm. She yanks back as if my fingers are flames licking her fucking skin and I instantly drop my hand.

Gritting my teeth I ask, "Who suggested it to you?"

She reaches inside the pocket of the black cargo pants she's wearing and takes out her phone. Thumbing the screen, she hands it to me without looking me in the eye. Yeah, I can't stand to look at myself in the mirror either, sweetness.

Glancing down I check the message on the screen and shake my head.

"Figures," I grunt and step toward my prez to

show him the message his mother sent to Ginny.

"Motherfucker," Archer rumbles once again.

I surprise myself by saying, "Mind if I take lead on this?"

"Fine." He rises from his chair and leans in to whisper, "My mother might have pushed her our way, but we have not received an official go-ahead. I don't need any vigilante shit nor does she. We do owe her one for working with us on the case where we almost lost you." He huffs out a curse. "Just don't get yourself killed and for fuck's sake, keep her from digging herself a hole she can't climb out of."

"You got it, Prez," I quip.

"Oh, and you're fully back I presume?" he questions.

I shoot him a grin. "Hell yes."

Now he's the one grinning. "Good. Glad to have you back. Work's been piling up." He hands me a thick file. "You're solo on this one."

"Thanks," I grunt and shove the file under my arm.

Stalking past Ginny, I tell her, "Follow me, please."

I grab my bag from the main room and head down the hall in the direction of my room. Opening the door, I step back to let her enter before me and close the door behind us. I throw my bag on the bed and glance around the empty room that looks the exact way I left it two months ago; neat and clean.

I can't resist and thumb through the file Archer gave me when I ask Ginny, "Mind telling me why Lynn thought you should swing by the clubhouse?"

There's no reason for me to ask why Lynn is texting her. Archer took over the gavel from his father years ago and at the time his mother was the president's old lady. The strong woman might be retired, but she still manages to stick her nose into everything. Even though she's moved with her husband to Ryckerdan.

She came to visit me at the hospital right after I woke up from the medically induced coma they put me in so my body could heal from the severe injuries I sustained. That's how she knows Ginny because the woman refused to leave me until she knew I was going to live.

"Mind giving me your full attention instead of going over another case? You know what? Never mind. The third time's a charm." She spins around and is set to leave.

I throw the file in the direction of the bed and move forward to block the door instead of touching her.

Releasing a deep sigh I admit, "You're right, I should have given you my full attention. Please. Sit and explain."

Instead of listening she backs up and crosses her arms in front of her chest before she starts to rattle. "Yesterday I went shopping and when I threw my bags into the trunk, I noticed a patrol car parking next to me. The agent behind the wheel he–" She swallows hard. "It was him."

Him. The one who ordered her kidnapping. Well, not her kidnapping, the fucker just wanted a female cop to do with as he pleases; he abused her. Forced his–

"It's okay." Her soft voice sounds close enough for her warm breath to feather over my chest.

I open my eyes and realize I've closed them in an effort to shove down the white-hot rage racing through me at the thought of her coming face-to-face with that fucker.

"It's not okay. Nothing is o-fucking-kay," I bark, making her flinch.

I step around her and mutter, "Sorry," and plunk down on the bed to take my head in my hands. So much for having my shit together and wanting to go back to work. Not even a few minutes back and I'm lashing out at the one person who doesn't deserve it.

The one woman I thought I'd never see again. I mean, we lived in the same town before this shit went down, but we never crossed paths before she was kidnapped. Then our worlds collided and she stayed by my bed for days until I was awake. When I finally woke up, I found out she left and didn't return. The day after that I contacted Archer and asked him to make arrangements for me to recover in Ryckerdan.

The bed dips beside me and I turn to face her. "Have you talked to anyone about what happened?"

She purses her lips and gives a small shake of her head. "I don't need to talk about what happened. It won't do me any good." She shrugs. "I'm not broken or damaged, but Archer is right about revenge being blinding." Her voice turns into a mere whisper when she adds, "Some days it's all I see."

Without thinking I place my forearm on my thigh and slide my hand–palm up–in her direction. She laces her fingers with mine and a full-body shiver runs through me at the mere touch. Fuck. The first time I saw her it was her mere presence that hit my chest like a wrecking ball.

Talking to her, touching her…being inside her. Fucking hell. Heaven and hell rolled into one because we did have a choice and yet we didn't. Fucked-up circumstances are all we had. If we had met any other time I'd make her mine without so much of a second thought. Silence wraps around us and she slowly leans her arm against mine and places her head on my shoulder.

"I've missed you," she whispers. "Funny. We've only been together a handful of hours and you practically went nuts when you saw me sitting next to your hospital bed and couldn't move to get to me. So much so that the nurses made me leave. They banned me from your room. I'm sorry I caused you so much pain. You shouldn't have–"

"Shut up," I croak and turn to face her. "You left. You left and didn't return."

Getting to my feet I start to pace and jerk my hand through my hair. "I don't remember going nuts. They shouldn't have made you leave. I didn't want you to leave."

"I didn't want to leave either," she states matter-of-factly. "You left too."

I lace my fingers together behind my neck and tip my head back to stare at the ceiling. "I had to go. I needed to recover and couldn't do it with my parents doting on me. My thoughts were all over the place and with the things I made you do–"

My leather cut is being yanked and I stare down at her fierce, honey-colored eyes. "You didn't make me do anything. I asked and you gave me a gift to obliterate the things I had to endure while they held me captive. You gave me hope. You almost gave your damn life for me, Arrow. I still can't believe we're standing here now."

She slides her arms around my waist and places her cheek against my chest. Serenity covers me like a blanket, and I engulf her with my body, pulling her closer and burying my nose into her hair to breathe her in.

I have no clue how long we stay this way, but our connection breaks when she says, "Why do you have an arson case to investigate? Doesn't the ATF take those cases?"

"Broken Deeds handles cases given to us by the government. Cold cases or some that are either hard to solve, lack evidence, suspicion of other agents involved, a connection that can't be made…loads of reasons and it doesn't matter what it involves since we specialize in every department. Archer handed me an arson case because I'm an EMT firefighter."

Her eyes widen. "I thought you were an agent."

"I'm also a tattoo artist." I chuckle. "It's a hard balance, but we're a tight brotherhood. The tattoo shop is owned by the club. My sister works there, as does Archer, and a few more brothers. I can drop everything when I'm on call. My father is now retired, but he was an EMT firefighter as well. I'm still on medical leave, but I'm resigning. Haven't told my parents yet, though I'm sure they'll understand. These past two months gave me a lot of time to think about things."

Not to mention, I need to take a physical to get cleared for duty. It might have been two months, but I'm still recovering. In my mind I'm fairly sure I'll pass, and my body might cooperate and yet I don't feel ready to do the job and that right there is a loud warning bell. So, retirement is a better choice for me.

"Yeah." She sighs. "Having enough time on your hands gives you the opportunity to let your body heal, and yet your mind runs on overtime."

"Why don't you attend your appointments with the psychiatrist?" I question. "You know they won't let you back to work without the psychiatrist's clearance."

Her voice is small when she repeats my words,

"I'm still on medical leave, but I'm resigning."

"Those are my words, Ginny." I grind my teeth. "Sounds like you just decided it on a damn whim. Why?"

She abruptly creates a large gap between our bodies. "I don't owe you or anyone an explanation." Her eyes stray to the file on the bed. "It's best if I leave now. You have enough on your plate as it is, even if you quit one of your three jobs."

"You haven't told me shit about why you came here. Other than you discovering the identity of the other man who put you through hell."

Ginny shrugs. "Nothing more to tell. I brought all the details and information to my chief's attention, and he told me to go home. He gave me the impression that he doesn't believe me. It seems people think I'm looking for a scapegoat. All while I'm one hundred percent sure it's the guy who forced his cock down my throat multiple times and gripped my hair to force me to stare into his eyes while he did so. Believe me when I say that fucker's face is branded on my corneas."

I release a string of curses at the reminder of what she went through.

"Your president has all the details, as does my chief. Do with it as you please." She spins on her heel and is bound to walk out of my door.

"Wait just one fucking second, Ginny," I growl. "Let me at least put my number into your phone. I'll look into this and make sure it won't be swept under the rug, okay? And if you think of something." I pause from putting my number into her phone and connect our gaze. "Call me. Anytime. You don't need a reason, okay? I'm here for you no matter what."

She takes her phone back and tucks it into her pocket. The sad smile she gives me tugs at my heart-strings.

Especially when she firmly states, "I can't expect you to be my hero each and every time, Arrow."

My chest tightens when she walks down the hall. I'm torn between going after her and calling out her name but in the end? I remain silent and rooted to the floor. Yet…she deserves so much more.

CHAPTER TWO

GINNY

A frustrating breath rips from my body. This is crazy. I should be able to go into my house without being paranoid. Every damn time I get home it takes me at least twenty minutes to talk myself off an emotional ledge.

I have no recollection of being kidnapped, but I instinctively know it must have happened somewhere between getting home or stepping into my house. For the first few weeks after I got home, my mother moved in with me and it made coming home a little more bearable instead of being alone.

She passed away in her sleep three weeks ago.

I miss her. A lot. Another reminder I'm all alone without anyone having my back. Reaching down, I touch the small handgun sitting on my hip. It's my backup gun and I touch my Glock that's in my shoulder holster, hidden under my jacket.

One more glance to make sure no one is around to catch me by surprise and I'm finally able to step out of my car. Maybe they're right. Maybe I should talk to a psychiatrist. My mother tried to seek help from a therapist after we escaped my biological father.

He was very abusive and even after decades my mother still had nightmares. Talking about it to some stranger sure didn't help her. A good alarm system and moving across the country did soothe some of the rough edges but she still reacted poorly to loud sounds, to name something. I guess in the end you simply learn to adjust and hope some triggers fade.

One can only hope, and that right there is my goal. I take a deep breath and jog up the steps to get to the door but freeze in my tracks. A quick glance around gives me the knowledge that I'm still alone and I retrace my steps until I'm back in my car and lock the doors.

My phone is in my hand, ready to call the emergency number, but they might think I'm crazy. What's there to say? A piece of tape isn't where I left it? They'd probably wave me off and blame it on paranoia due to recent experiences.

But I'm not crazy nor paranoid, dammit. Whenever I go out, I place a small piece of tape on the door–strategically placed to make sure it's not obvious–and now it's gone. Which means…someone went inside. But how do I explain this? And what if the mail carrier or the neighborhood kid ripped it off? No. It wouldn't be gone unless someone went inside. My breathing picks up and I hold the phone tighter.

"I'm not crazy," I croak.

A sob escapes and I risk a glance in the direction of the house. Maybe I should check into a hotel for the night? My phone vibrates in my hand, and I notice it's a message from Arrow, asking if I got home okay. I am home. But I'm not okay.

My fingers move over the screen and I hit send when I've typed out the words "I put tape on my door to make sure I can tell that no one enters while I'm not there. Now it's gone."

There. He already thinks I'm crazy, so what's the worst thing that can happen? A tiny scream rips from me when the phone instantly starts to ring. Holy shit. I'm on edge.

"Hello," I choke and whip my head around.

Paranoid much? Yeah. Definitely. Can't dodge that label with the reaction I just had.

"You didn't go inside, did you?" His voice sounds off and the roar of an engine lets me know he might have connected the call through his hands-free set if he's riding his bike.

"No. I went back to my car." I release another deep breath. "I'm paranoid. Maybe the wind or—"

"Fuck paranoid," Arrow growls. "Tell me where I'm going."

I rattle off my address.

"Good. Stay put, and lock your doors," he orders.

I wipe a stray tear from my cheek and try to calm

myself down. I've already made a fool out of myself in front of him once today, there's no need to add more drama to the train wreck that's me.

The rumbling of bikes draws my attention and two of them come down the street. One biker I recognize as Arrow, the other I have no clue who it might be. I met more than a few of them when Arrow was in the hospital. Arrow hits the kickstand and dismounts. He taps my window and I get out of my car.

"This is Stephan, one of my club brothers. Stay with him while I check out the house."

I bob my head, but he's already walking toward the door.

"Sorry you guys had to come out here. It's probably nothing," I muse and rub my temples, already feeling another headache building due to stress.

Stephan shifts and comes to stand next to me as we lean against my car.

"'It's probably nothing' most times turns into dangerous shit when it comes to us," he casually states. "Better to be safe than sorry is something everyone should live by."

"Ain't that the truth." I glance up to see Arrow stalking toward us.

He throws his thumb over his shoulder. "Mind walking through the house with me to see if anything is out of place?"

I step forward and follow Arrow as we check the house room by room. Everything is exactly the way it was when I left this morning. Until I get to the bedroom and notice the horrifying device lying on the floor in front of the mirror.

I stumble back and gasp. "No." The word sounds broken as it falls from my lips.

Arrow's gaze follows mine and he releases a string of curses when he sees the metal ring held by leather straps. It's designed to prevent your mouth from closing. I had never seen one before I was taken, but was forced to get acquainted with it real fast. It was used repeatedly by that fucked-up man who had me kidnapped.

He takes his phone from his pocket and hits the screen before placing it to his ear. "Prez. I have more than one reason to believe Ginny's house was breached. I need a team here to take some evidence with them, run prints, that kind of stuff. Yeah. No. I'll bring her back with me. Will do."

He ends the call and puts his phone away. "Are you okay to drive your own car?"

I bob my head.

"I'd ask you to pack a bag but as you might have heard I'm getting a team in here to run prints."

I shrug. "Ever since it happened, I have a bug-out bag along with a backpack with personal things. There's a set in the trunk of my car, another set in the closet behind you, and one in a storage unit down-town."

"Consider me impressed," Stephan murmurs be-hind me.

"Okay, let's retrace our steps and wait out front," Arrow orders.

Ten minutes later I'm following Arrow back to the clubhouse. Stephan stayed behind to oversee the team going through my house to take fingerprints and bag the open- mouth ring gag. Fun times. A wave of mortification hits me like a heated flare of nausea and I try to breathe through it.

I've experienced way worse. These men are professionals. They might seem like a bunch of outlaw bikers from the outside, but they work for the government and solve crime cases by using any means possible to gain justice. Not to mention, I might be on medical leave, but I am a freaking professional too, dammit.

Knocking on my window scares the shit out of me and I realize I've been staring out the front window while rambling to myself inside my head as I parked near the clubhouse. Shit. Ripping the keys from the ignition, I pop the trunk and step out of the car.

"There's no need for me to stay here. I could check into a hotel or something," I offer.

"Fat chance," Arrow snaps and points at a side road next to the clubhouse. "There are a few duplexes where the first generation lives, my parents included. My house is further down the road from them."

"Why do you have a room at the clubhouse when you have a house this close to the clubhouse?" I wonder out loud.

Arrow chuckles and takes the bags from the trunk when I was just about to grab them.

"Sometimes it's easier to stay there, but if I want quiet time to myself or to cook shit and so on? A place of my own is way better than a single room."

I bob my head as we stroll past the clubhouse. We both come to a stop when Archer appears along with Bee, his old lady.

"Arrow. Mind if we have a word?" Archer rumbles.

Arrow nods and jerks his chin in my direction. "Let me get her settled and I'll come find you."

Archer slowly shakes his head. "Right now." He glances at me. "Bee will keep you company."

"Thanks," I mutter and give Bee a kind smile.

Bee is one of the many old ladies I've spent time with. Not only at the hospital, but also after I cut ties with Arrow. The last time I saw her was at my mother's funeral where she showed up with Lynn and a few other old ladies.

I haven't returned any of their calls and texts because I feel I didn't belong with them due to their connection with Arrow. These folks have a tight brotherhood and family where they stand up for one another. I'm an outsider. The only reason why they kept in contact was because I helped them close a case and helped save Arrow's life. After he was injured saving me, I might add.

The guys leave and Bee points at the clubhouse. "Let's go inside where we can head into one of the rooms for some privacy and have a little chat."

I follow her into the clubhouse. "I'm sorry I didn't return your messages," I blurt.

Bee nods as she holds the door open. "I assumed you were busy, and still processing everything that happened over the past few months. The havoc you went through and losing your mother on top of it. I understand you feel disconnected and would want nothing more than to either crawl into your own shell or bury yourself in work. Something they won't allow you to do without the psychological clearance."

I snort. "You're hitting a little too close to home," I honestly admit.

"Have a seat." Bee points at a desk.

My gaze slides through the empty room which only holds a desk, a few chairs, and a mirror, and I can't help but blurt, "This looks like an interrogation room." Especially with the window disguised as a mirror that's obviously there so someone can follow what's going on inside this room.

"Sorry. It is." Bee takes a seat and places her phone in front of her. "So. Tell me. Why did you use your user ID and password to log in and run the information after you went to your chief? You were told to leave it alone, and that they would be following up on the things you reported. You do know they can easily check the log, right?"

I can't help wincing when she points out something I know damn well. For the first time, I voice the thoughts that have been running through my head ever since I ran into the asshole who had me kidnapped.

"Recognizing him? Finding out he's a cop?"

I shake my head. "There's no way I can go back to work now. After I talked to the chief, I knew he wouldn't let me come back to work either. The way he looked at me with pity?" I bark a humorless laugh. "Yeah, my career is over. I just know the chief wouldn't do anything, so I made sure I knew exactly who the asshole who did this to me was. It's only fair I now know his name is Fabio Kylen, where he lives, and the rest of the information showing in his file… because he knows exactly who I am."

Bee nods. "What would you do if you came face-to-face with him?"

Her question catches me by surprise. "What do you mean? If I run into Fabio Kylen? Come face- to-face with the man who faked being a biker and did–"

I clamp my mouth shut to prevent throwing out in the open how that man forced me to take his dick in my mouth. Repeatedly.

"Yes. What would happen if you would face the man who did all those things to you?"

I have to admit, there have been many moments over the past two months where every scenario ran through my mind. Especially thoughts where I carved every inch of flesh from his bones with a dull knife. But to have Bee ask me this question is somehow different.

Honesty is something I always stand by and it's why I give her the first thing that comes to mind. "If he pulled a gun on me, I'd kill him. If he was putting other people in danger, I'd kill him. If he didn't have a weapon on him and there wasn't any other risk I'd detain him and make sure he went to jail. I can only hope he'd turn into someone's bitch where he gets a dick in his mouth and ass a few times a day. Yes, killing him would be too easy. Can I take the first few comments back? I'd hit him in the knee or whatever to make sure he can't do any harm and then let him end up in jail. Death is too easy for scum like him."

"I told you she's sane. Now, clear her so she can help work the case that obviously isn't closed yet."

My gaze goes to the phone on the table where the voice is coming from.

"Lynn?" I ask, completely stunned she's on the phone and heard everything we just discussed.

"Yes, chickie. You didn't think I'd leave you hanging, did you? I told you at the funeral that you're not alone. I knew you weren't listening or accepting my words, so I had to make sure you were looked after. It's why I told you to give my son the information when you found out who that scumbag was who touched you." She releases a string of curses. "Sorry, that idiot kid of mine always plays by the rules. I don't remember raising him that way," she huffs. "Anyway, it's a good thing my daughter-in-law makes up for his flaws."

The door swings open. "Ma, what the fuck," Archer growls.

"Now those words, I did teach him."

Bee chuckles and quickly takes her phone in hand. "We'll talk later," she tells Lynn and ends the call.

"Next time, Prez? Don't expect me to simply stand by and let her face shit alone. You might not have given me a choice this time, but I swear to fuck I won't let you put me in the same position ever again." Arrow is suddenly standing next to me and holds his hand out for me to take. "Come on, Ginny. We're leaving."

I slide my palm over his and he pulls me from the chair.

"Arrow," Archer grits, but Arrow keeps walking.

"Arrow," Archer snaps.

Arrow whirls around and snaps, "What?"

"You know damn well we have to follow certain protocols. We might do things our way, but we still need to justify some shit. Now get your woman up to speed. And don't fucking forget about the other case I gave you."

"I won't forget," Arrow grits.

Though I'm fairly sure he isn't talking about the cases, but the fact that he won't forget what just went down. I don't even understand what the hell went down but I do know one thing...Arrow is pissed with a capital P.

We walk into his house a few minutes later and I instantly spot my bags on the couch in his living room. Someone must have brought them in while I was being interrogated. I still can't believe they put me through that and yet I understand in some way.

Arrow rubs the back of his neck and he mutters with a hint of sadness and pain in his voice, "I didn't know your mother died."

"Cardiac arrest. She died in her sleep," I absently tell him. "Lynn, Bee, and a few of the other old ladies showed up at the funeral. Lynn obviously stayed in touch and if I don't reply, she simply keeps spamming me with messages until I do. It's why I spilled my guts to her when I left the station after reporting Fabio to my chief. She told me to relay the information to her son."

He sinks down into one of the chairs. "I can't believe Lynn didn't tell me. If I'd known…I would have returned sooner."

I shrug, not really knowing what to say to that.

He releases a frustrated breath. "The whole interrogation thing wasn't my idea."

"I figured with the both of them blocking our path and pulling us apart and into separate rooms." I take a seat across from him. "Listen. You don't owe me anything, Arrow. I'm thankful at least someone is willing to check into things."

"Fabio Kylen's alibi checks out according to your chief," Arrow blurts.

Shock hits me and it causes my breath to catch. "No. That's impossible. His alibi is lying. Who is his alibi?"

"His brother." Arrow keeps his gaze pinned on mine when he adds, "There's a video of them walking into a bar and the owner of the bar also has a camera on the inside. It only brings a small part of the bar into view because he was trying to catch a bartender stealing cash, but it shows the brothers heading for a table. Fabio isn't in the feed at all times, but his brother is. Hours later the two of them walk out again."

I swallow hard to keep the bile from rising in my throat. There's no mistake, I recognized him. No doubt at all, Fabio is the one who abused me. I'm not imagining things nor pointing my finger at some innocent cop to find a scapegoat. On the other hand, how is it possible for him to be in two places at the same time? It's clearly not possible…but I know–know damn sure–he's my abuser.

"That was one time he had an alibi," I croak. "The second time he–"

Arrow shakes his head. "Same alibi, same occurrence on the video."

I jolt to my feet. "That's impossible."

"Archer and Ganza checked into it and one time would presume a solid alibi, but with both being at the same bar, them sitting at the same table, and Fabio missing from the feed…it's questionable. In any other case, it would be your word against his, and not much evidence to go on. Since we're already involved, and this case is tied to the one we just solved, and having inside information…we are standing on your side instead of backing up a cop."

"I'm still a cop too, even if I'm on medical leave," I grumble under my breath.

"I thought you wanted to resign?" he fires back without missing a beat.

I glare at the annoying man.

The corner of his mouth twitches. "You passed

the test and my president would like you to once again help us out. It concerns the case that clearly wasn't closed the day we got you out of the fucked-up situation you were thrown in. Are you up for working with us, with me, again?"

Relief floods my veins. "Hell yes, I'm in," I practically squeal in excitement. Toning it somewhat down I question, "Am I even technically allowed to be involved? I mean, I'm practically a part of the case and not so much a witness, but more of a victim. Things will never hold up in court if we do manage to nail Fabio."

"That's why Lynn suggested Bee question you on tape. There will also be some paperwork you'll need to sign and I'm your partner for the unforeseeable future. Meaning you won't be leaving my side."

My eyes practically bulge out of my head. "How is that going to work?"

"We'll bunk together from now on. Besides, your house was compromised and I'll sleep better anyway by knowing you're safe under my roof on the private property of Broken Deeds MC." The man shrugs as if it's no big deal.

"We can't live and work together," I snap.

Not after what we went through–what we had to do while being undercover the last time–and Arrow almost losing his life in the end. The way he lashed out at me in the hospital room after he woke up from the medically induced coma they put in. Then the medical staff banned me, him leaving for months, and returning without a word.

Add his reaction upon seeing me in Archer's office and all the pieces fall together.

It's a mere whisper when I state, "It's a bad idea. Especially since you don't even like me."

CHAPTER THREE

ARROW

If there's anything further from the truth, it's the statement she just threw into this fucked-up world.

"What the fuck?" I growl. "Whatever gave you the damn idea that I don't like you?"

She blinks a few times.

Her voice lacks her normal feistiness when she says, "Your actions did." Her shoulders sag. "I'm sorry if I misunderstood. Maybe I did somewhat paint you off as a hero inside my head and got kicked in the back once I was back out. But you gave me hope at the darkest time in my life. I didn't see a way out other than death. Then there was you. Your proposition…I shouldn't have asked you to… to–"

She clears her throat in an effort to find words to describe how she asked–no, begged–me to make love to her. Fuck. My chest squeezes while my cock jerks inside my pants. It was the most intense sex of my life and it was fucking missionary. Nothing special except for the worshiping words I kept whispering in her ear.

They brought her into that room for me to do with as I pleased. I paid fifteen grand to do whatever I wanted. I could have fucked her raw, sliced her up, and damn well killed her all for the amount of cash I paid those fuckers. We had a cover to uphold if we wanted to bring all those fuckers down.

Yet, I left that room barren and raw. She shredded me with the tears sliding down her cheeks due to momentary pleasure. Pleasure we gave one another of our own free will. She fucking thanked me for honoring her request. She could have agreed to let me save her, but she insisted to go back so we could save all women involved; future and present.

Sacrifices. Scars run deep in those who are painfully aware of the torment running through our veins. Yet, we–and many others working in law enforcement and other connected professions–choose to put others before ourselves no matter how big the stains on our soul get because of it.

I chose Ginny. Willingly. While she chose everyone else before herself. What we did was in some form expected to keep our cover intact, but it was much more. So fucking much more.

It's why I tap my temple with one finger and snap, "You're in here." My hand curls into a fist. I punch my chest, and cup myself as I snarl, "My cock was inside you. And it was your pussy rippling with pleasure twice before you took me over the edge with you. So don't fucking stand there and state that I don't like you. I damn well admire you for your strength, your captivating beauty, sweet curves, and that sassy mouth of yours." I bark a laugh that lacks humor. "How can you say I don't like you when all I want to do is take back our first time together so I can share it with you now? Without everything or anyone tainting it."

Fuck. I didn't mean for all of that to just pour out of me. She looks as stunned as I am.

Clearing my throat, I softly tell her, "I guess we both misunderstood and misplaced actions. I wasn't myself when I woke up because I'd never with a sane mind would have wanted you to leave. I left to recover in Ryckerdan so I could escape everything and everyone because you weren't there."

"Talk about one huge misunderstanding," Ginny mutters.

We sink down into our seats and let silence wrap around us. Both processing the things we just shared.

Or so I thought because she surprises the fuck out of me when she says, "We should draw a line."

"A line?" I echo and frown, trying to understand what she means by this.

"Yes. Draw a line and leave every misunderstanding, misplaced action, and whatever happened in our past. A clean start. Neither of us chose any of it. We were thrown together and did what we could to get the best outcome. I guess we succeeded because we're both standing here, alive and well. That counts for something, right?"

I feel a smile slide across my face. "Did I add in my admittance of adoration that you were smart?"

The corner of her mouth twitches. "I believe you left that one out, but thanks for adding it on second thought."

"You're welcome." I grin. "Now, would you like to see the video and the rest of the information we've gathered so far?"

Her eyes flare. "Yes. Definitely. But don't you need to work on the other case as well? The arson one?"

"Yes." I rise from my seat. "Why don't we order some food and multitask? You can check the video and the other info while I read through my other case. Then we'll discuss things after we both have a chance to work by ourselves."

"Sounds good," she agrees.

I grab my phone and shoot a text to a prospect after we agreed to have some sushi. We're both going through files when there's a knock on the door. I take the food and hand the prospect some cash.

Ginny doesn't even look up when I place the food on the table; she's completely engrossed in the details of the case. She takes the chopsticks I offer her and dives into the food. We eat in silence for a few long minutes.

Her eyes find mine and she asks, "Do you guys hack into every system to check things? Like, for instance, if you wanted to see if there were dead bodies in the surrounding cities, reported kidnappings, missing persons, check someone's financial records, do a background check on a spouse, how far is your reach and are you all really above the law?"

"I could tell you, but then you'd have to become my old lady," I tell her with a straight face.

Her eyes bulge and then they dance with laughter when she says, "You almost had me there. Okay, so it's an 'I can tell you, but then I'd have to kill you' thing. Figures. I was just wondering since it's kinda mind-boggling how everything went the last time. I never really thought about anything when I was right in the middle of it. But the months after you were hurt, I wondered how there was a chopper in the blink of an eye to fly you to the nearest hospital. Kessie already being there when we landed and taking over like she owned the damn place. Like I said, at the time I didn't think about it, but it's all kinda weird."

"We close cases," I simply tell her. "We do have some rules to follow, but there's basically no limit to our abilities and resources. That doesn't mean we can do whatever the fuck we want...though it sure comes close to it."

"That's good," she muses. "In some cases, the hands of the law are tied to legal procedures. Victims are left in the cold while criminals are celebrating behind barriers that give them freedom." She huffs a frustrated breath and shoves the papers lying in front of her back into the file. "This is bullshit. I can't find anything to go on that might connect Fabio to a crime. Other than being a witness to it myself."

I take the file from her and throw it further away from us. "What you need is a palette cleanser. Let your mind focus on something else and come morning we'll discuss over breakfast and see if we can come up with a few leads to run."

Handing her a few photographs of the arson case, I start to explain. "Three houses were set on fire, roughly two to three weeks apart from one another. Fires happen, but these all had traces of accelerant used and all of them started at the back of the house, near the master bedroom." I took a few documents in my hand and showed her some more photographs. "One woman died, two other homeowners are still alive but suffered severe burns."

"Any suspects? All three random?" she muses. "Something tells me this pyromaniac won't stop until he's caught."

"No clues, no connection whatsoever. Except for the origin of the fire is the same at all three houses."

Ginny takes the documents in hand and glances over them. "Single females. All of them. Maybe a guy? Jerking off while staring into the bedroom and using fire to cover it up while it escalates into a fire?"

Stunned, I blink a few times to process her words. "Now that's a theory that hasn't crossed my mind yet."

The corner of her mouth twitches and she gives me her honey-colored eyes. "That's because my mind works differently than yours. Besides, with the things I endured I now probably only think the dirty and worst of men before thinking of more normal options."

The casual twitch of laughter disappears, letting a frown slide in place instead as she stares down at the table. Dammit. She might consider herself strong and doesn't want to talk to anyone about it, but it's clear she's still struggling.

I rise from my seat and hold out my hand. "Come on."

She doesn't think twice and slides her fingers over my palm. "Where are we going?"

A grin slides across my face and a surge of pride warms my chest at the knowledge of her trust in me; giving me her hand to come with me before asking where we're going.

"For a ride," I merely tell her.

I grab my leather coat and hold it out for her. She

slides her arms through the holes and takes over to zip up.

"We need to swing by my parents," I grumble and lead her out the door.

She doesn't question me and I'm also thankful my parents aren't home when I snatch my mother's helmet. Ginny gives me a small smile when I strap it on.

"We need to buy you one of your own." I straddle my bike and offer her my hand.

Once again, her fingers slide over my palm as she slides on behind me. I give her some quick instructions and she instantly follows them. I have no clue what I was thinking when I suggested we should go for a ride. Especially now that she's plastered against me, pussy and tits up close and personal. Not to mention, her hands are locked together mere inches from my cock.

Why did I think going for a ride would be good for both of us? The feeling of having her close surges through my mind. Skin to skin, whispered words, hands roaming, how good her pussy felt wrapped around my cock.

"Everything okay?" Ginny whispers in a hot breath beside my ear, her chin resting on my shoulder.

I swallow hard. "Ready to ride?"

My cock preferably, I mentally add. Something I'd rather do at this point than ride around town with a damn boner that can cut through damn wood. That's how hard the reminder of being inside her makes me.

Her arms tighten around me. "I'll always be ready for whatever you have in mind."

Motherfucker. What kind of perfect answer was that? Did she hear my inner thoughts? Trying not to let it get to me, I fire up my bike and hit the road. Night has fallen and at this time of day, there isn't much traffic.

I ride for over half an hour, enjoying the calm setting in my bones. Trees flashing by, no weight or obligations pressing down on me, except for focusing on riding. The sensation of Ginny warming my back is an empowering feeling.

I knew she was damn special when I picked her from a mere image, only to find out she was a rookie cop. Then meeting her face-to-face and having her agree to work undercover together. Her begging me to give her an escape in the form of lovemaking.

She's so damn strong. A rock standing proud above sea level as the waves keep crashing against it; a sight to behold. To hear her say, and think, that I don't like her? Fuck. It's the complete opposite.

Another twenty minutes later and I'm parking in front of my house.

She jumps off and is working the straps of her helmet when she gushes, "Oh my gosh. I am sooooo getting lessons to ride myself. That was freaking amazing. Can we do it again tomorrow?"

A chuckle slips free as we head inside my house. "We sure can. Like I said, we need to buy you your own helmet."

She kicks off her shoes and I do the same.

"Did you want to go through the cases again?" she questions me.

I find myself shaking my head. "Nah. How about

a drink and a movie? Relax before we get some sleep. As I said, we'll get back to it tomorrow morning with fresh eyes and minds."

"Sounds good. What movie did you have in mind?"

"Let's scroll and see what we can both agree on," I offer.

We settle in and she curls her bare feet under her ass. I throw my arm over the back of the couch and grab the remote. I'm flipping through movies for a few minutes when I feel the weight of her body sink against me.

Glancing down I watch how she slowly moves until her head is in my lap. Her eyes are closed and she snuggles a bit to make herself comfortable. I grab the blanket that's draped over the back of the couch and throw it over her body. I hit play on a documentary and feel utterly content. So much so that I fall asleep right along with her.

Content is not what I feel when I am roused from my sleep with the nagging feeling of being watched.

"I told you they're cute together," Lynn's voice

filters through my brain. "They both needed time to heal, enough to move forward together."

"You were right," I hear my mother say. "As always."

Lynn chuckles and I have to blink a few times at the phone my mother is holding out. She's fucking FaceTiming Lynn so she can see me and Ginny sleeping together in a heap on the damn couch.

"What the fuck, Ma?" I groan.

My mother and Lynn exchange a quick goodbye and then my mother bends forward to shove a plate that's sitting on the table closer to me.

"I thought I'd bring you two some breakfast," she innocently tells me.

Ginny stirs on my lap. She slowly sits up and stretches, arms into the air and a grunt leaves her. She starts to yawn and covers her mouth with her hand when she glances at me and then at my mother. Her attention slides to the plate between us and she leans in to check and takes a whiff.

"Oh my gosh. Syrniki?" she asks with hope tainting her voice.

"Yes," my mother answers. "Good guess."

Ginny grins. "Not a guess, I recognized the Russian pancakes my father used to make. It's been years since I've had them. He taught me how to make them, but I never seem to get them the way he used to do."

"Your father is Russian?" my mother questions.

Ginny takes the plate and moves toward the kitchen. "My grandfather was. He moved here when he tried to escape the mafia. He was an informant and worked hard to become some sort of consultant for law enforcement. Also, the reason why my father became a cop, with me following in his footsteps. So, not really but there is some in my background. Hence the love for these things." She holds up the plate and shoots me a look over her shoulders. "Sorry, Arrow. I won't be sharing since it's your mom who made them and you can get more. I'm going to treasure these."

She disappears into the kitchen and I bark out a laugh.

My mother chuckles. "I like her."

I roll my eyes. "You approve knowing she has a hint of Russian," I tease.

I know all about my mother's background. Once upon a time, she was a mafia princess. Her father was the head of a large mafia gang. Her father stepped down and gave the leadership to a guy named Ford, stepping away for the sake of his daughter and retired. The fucker even ran off with Archer's great-grandmother.

Yeah, my father knocked up a mafia princess. Funny story since they met when my mother saved my half-sister, Hadley. They were at the zoo and she tumbled right into the water. They were both soaked and my dad brought her home. They had a quickie in the hallway and he left.

Hit and run so to say and my mother showed up at the clubhouse when she found out she was pregnant. My dad claimed her on the spot and they've been happily together ever after since. Sure, they had loads of shit to deal with 'cause life's never easy, but their love and relationship have reinforced walls no bullshit can penetrate.

It's actually something I've always wanted for myself. Knowing it's out there makes you not want to settle for less. The way my body responds to Ginny, how our lives were thrown together and two months later we cross paths again...now knowing she has a love for Syrniki?

Practically the same reaction my dad had when my mom made them for him. Not wanting to share since she stole them just now and disappeared into the kitchen and hasn't returned since. Yeah, I can take a hint when life gives me pointers to follow.

If she's up for exploring what might be between us? I'm all in. 'Cause I've slept a solid five hours on the couch with her in one night. That's more than I usually get in three days.

"I'll go check if she inhaled everything or if she's left some for me," I tell my mom.

My mother chuckles. "No worries, son. I'll make some more or teach her how to make them properly. Now, was that my helmet I saw in the hallway?"

I wince. "Sorry. I had a spur-of-the-moment thought to take her for a ride and didn't have an extra helmet. We'll buy one for her today."

My mother is grinning ear to ear. "You can have this one. It's my spare anyway." She closes the distance between us and gives me a hug. "I'm happy for you, sweetie. She's a gem."

My father calls my mother Diamond because she is one. In his words, "First there's carbon, black... like the shiny darkness surrounding that gorgeous head of hers. Diamond is the most concentrated form of pure carbon." So that's why he calls his old lady by the name of her beauty that captured him.

That's what he always tells her and for my mother to call Ginny a gem? Yeah, for sure she's a damn precious gemstone. One who stands out between the gravel, whose beauty captured me at first sight.

CHAPTER FOUR

GINNY

I swallow a forkful of Syrniki down and watch Arrow stroll into the kitchen along with his mother.

"You made a fresh strawberry sauce to go with it," I practically croak. "I could cry, you know that? It's delicious and I have no clue why I'm this emotional. Maybe because I've slept through the night for the first time in months or the fact I'm tasting something that reminds me of home...family." I scoop up some more delicious bites of food and hold it in front of my mouth. "Speaking of family...I probably shouldn't have mentioned the mafia tie in my family tree." I wince. "It only adds to the dark and crazy clinging to me. You guys being full-blown law enforcement, working for the government, and doing above and beyond to gain justice… maybe it will–"

"Oh, honey," Diamond softly says and chuckles as she takes a seat at the kitchen table right next to me. "Don't worry about your reputation or how people here see or treat you after finding out you have a mafia connection tucked far away in your past." She leans in closer. "Speaking from personal experience, I can tell you it means shit to them. Once upon a time, I was a mafia princess. Lost my virginity the day I fell pregnant with Arrow. His father and I had the kind of chemistry you can't deny. It hit hard and fast and we parted ways the same day. I didn't even know his name, only the name of his daughter, and the motorcycle club he was a part of since it was on his leather cut. At the time he had Hadley, his daughter, to fully focus on since he had only recently gained custody of her. With Hadley being deaf it was a lot of adjusting for both father and daughter. Depay also had to learn sign language, to both interpret and speak. In the end, I was the one who went looking for him when I found out I was pregnant."

"That was the day I claimed her and never let go," Depay rumbles as he steps into the kitchen. "Best day and choice of my life. I should have gone back for her sooner 'cause the woman never left my mind since I met her. Funny how life found a way to tie us together anyway."

He walks over to where his wife is sitting and leans in while at the same time cupping his wife's neck so she has no other option than to take his fierce and dominating kiss. I let out a little swoony sigh. I know it's not a word but there's no other way to describe their love shining bright and the longing it creates within me to have something similar.

"It was all Arrow, demanding to be a part of this world." Depay chuckles when his wife tells him that with a grumble, though her face shows all the love. "Also, the reason you picked his name before he was even born."

"Yup," Depay quips. "Arrow never misses his mark, because he hits home in one go." He glances at his son. "The fucker still does with everything in life."

I find Arrow staring right at me, determination on his face as if he just realized something, and grunts, "Damn right."

Not knowing what to say to any of it, I simply polish off the rest of my breakfast.

"Prez asked me to swing by and tell you to answer your phone or check your messages," Depay tells Arrow.

Arrow curses and pulls his phone from his pocket. "Gotta check in," he mutters and leaves the kitchen.

"Thanks for the amazing breakfast." I give Arrow's mother a huge smile.

She grins at me. "You're very welcome, sweetie. You know where to find me when you want to make them together."

"She loves them as much as I do, huh?" Depay rumbles and glances my way. "I never want to share them either."

"She more than loves them. It's a piece of home since her father used to make them for and with her.

They might have been born and raised in the US, but her grandfather was Russian," Diamond explains for me.

"What a damn coincidence," Depay mutters.

Diamond grins. "Need I mention her grandfather had mafia ties and came here to escape them and work with law enforcement?"

"Fuck. More than a coincidence...sounds fucking familiar." He reaches out and caresses his wife's cheek.

I'm still shamelessly soaking up their loving connection when Arrow stomps back into the kitchen.

"There's been another fire." His eyes connect with mine. "Wanna freshen up and head over there with me?"

I rise from my seat. "Sure thing."

It takes a few minutes to dash into the bathroom with my bag and quickly handle my business and change into some fresh, clean clothes. I don't bother with makeup, but splash some water on my face and only have to slide my fingers through my hair.

Doing my hair used to be a full-blown routine.

Cutting it short was a spur-of-the-moment decision I don't regret. Instant relief hit me to know it wasn't long enough for anyone to grab and drag me around. Some fears I can cope with and eliminate, the way I cut my hair for one. Others are a bit harder to cope with.

I need total quiet to sleep and not full lights on, only the bathroom or hallway lights. This way I can hear if something is coming and can hide when I need to. Mental scars. Maybe I should talk to a psychiatrist, but I never was one to talk or share my feelings for that matter.

"Ready," I quip as I stalk into the living room.

Arrow hands me his mother's helmet. "She told me she had another one so we're good to keep this for you until we can buy a new one."

I merely nod. There's no need to remind him of the fact that I don't have a motorcycle and won't be here with him long-term. I wish I was, though. Yesterday I discovered that I loved being on the back of his bike.

Learning to ride is definitely going on my bucket

list. After being kidnapped and held for days, I swore to myself to do stuff if I did manage to survive. I have weird stuff on my mental bucket list, but after Arrow entered my life I definitely added "sex like that," to the number one spot.

Damn, that man made me feel. Alive, worshipped, special, cherished...he simply made me feel. After that fucker Fabio degraded me–by repeatedly putting me bound and on my knees with an open ring gag so he could fuck my mouth–I needed an escape.

Arrow gave it to me, yet his reaction at the hospital and now gives me the impression that I might have asked too much of him. I know I shouldn't have, though when he explained who he was and why he was there I knew we needed to have sex or at least do something.

Otherwise, we would've risked getting caught or maybe made them aware Arrow had other motives by not touching me. It doesn't matter anyway. It's in the past now and I can't do anything to change it. I am glad we talked about it and agreed to draw a line.

Strangely enough, I have no clue how to proceed

from here on out. Friends would be nice, but knowing how good he made me feel at the darkest moment in my life is something I'm unable to forget.

He gently squeezes my thigh, indicating I should get off the bike. See? He has the ability to sweep me away. Ever since I was kidnapped and saved I haven't been able to relax, let alone lower my guard.

With Arrow near, though? I can sleep for hours and even daydream. Yeah, screw friends. If the man would ask me to marry him, I wouldn't walk to the courthouse, I'd freaking run like my ass is on fire.

"If you have any questions, ask. I'm not a mind reader and I tend to take in the scene and work everything out in my head so I don't talk all that much. Doesn't mean I'm ignoring you," Arrow rambles as we walk to a man in a firefighter uniform. "I gotta go talk to the chief."

He doesn't give me a chance to so much as acknowledge his words as he offers his hand to the firefighter.

"Chief," Arrow grunts.

"Rooney, sad to hear you're leaving now that

you're finally back in town," the chief tells him.

Arrow's face doesn't show any emotion when he states, "It's only been a little over two months. My body might look healed, but it's also only been two months. Meaning I could jump into a run, though not as long and fast as before I got shot. Let alone do it with the needed gear and equipment."

Shit. That asshole. He gave me a whole different reason why he was quitting and what he's saying to his chief clearly states he's giving up his job because he was injured. Because of me.

"You can take some more time off," the chief starts.

Arrow shakes his head. "It won't change my mind. I'm going to focus on new challenges. One of them being my old lady."

He holds out his hand and I'm stunned but slide my fingers over his palm without thinking, letting him pull me against his body.

"This here is Ginny, my old lady," Arrow announces and instead of meeting the chief I find myself staring up at the man who practically introduced me as his freaking girlfriend.

No. Not just girlfriend. What I've heard about all the biker lingo from the old ladies is that this claim is similar to being married…biker style. I shake my head and turn to the chief. Arrow must have his reasons for this insane pretend scheme.

I shake the man's hand and Arrow tells me, "Can you glance around? I'm going to discuss the details some more and will find you later."

"Sure," I mutter and quickly step away from them.

My mind is still boggling as I take my time to glance around the scene. There's a bit of a crowd who is staring at the house which is now drenched with water. Firefighters are still walking in and out and the majority of the people are behind the tape they secured around the scene.

One woman draws my attention and it's all because she's wearing a neon green sweater. Man, that's not easy on the eyes. I can't believe she has huge, thick hoops in her ears to match the freaking sweater. Her blonde curls bounce in the wind.

If I think her appearance is weird, then the look she is wearing definitely sparks my attention. It's as if she's enjoying the view. I grab my phone and take a short video of all the people watching.

"Ready to check out the origin of the fire?" Arrow asks from beside me, making me jump.

He curses under his breath. "Sorry."

I shove my phone back into my pocket and face him. "Did the chief mention any details that were different from the others?"

Arrow places his hand on my lower back and guides me around the house as he gives me a short recap of what he found out. It's frustrating and creepy to hear how these cases have so many similarities.

"This time the woman had a knife in her chest," Arrow mutters as he squats down to examine the origin of the fire. "Chief said the windows upstairs were opened."

"Why?" I wonder.

He lifts his head my way. "Means the arsonist started the fire here and made sure to give it loads of oxygen by ventilating this building at the top. This causes the fire to race upwards and quickly spread, rather than to keep it to just this room."

"Damn," I mutter. "So, does this mean the arsonist is a firefighter? I mean, I don't have knowledge of how this works and I'm a cop. He must be obsessed with fire."

Arrow slowly rises to his full length. "Why do you think it's a man?"

I shrug, thinking back to what happened to me and how Fabio degraded me, the things he said. Fuck. The things he said. I've blocked it all, not to be reminded by it, but this does make me realize something.

"Because the victims are all female. All single females, right? Maybe the arsonist is a pissed off nutcase whom these women turned down or something," I muse and add on a second thought, "Maybe something we should also check about Fabio."

Arrow gives me a confused look. "Fabio? I don't think these two cases are connected."

"No, I mean we should check if Fabio has done the same thing to other women as he did with me.

If he had women, girlfriends, or whatever, who he abused. Maybe even assaulted and they never reported it because he's a cop?"

"Smart thinking," Arrow grunts and takes a small notebook from his leather cut to scribble something in it before he tucks it away. "We'll check later. For now, we have to focus on this case."

"Did anyone question the women who survived if they were dating someone? A stalker maybe?"

He slightly tilts his head. "You're liking the man slash stalker slash boyfriend angle, huh?"

"I'm just throwing around ideas. I mean, location doesn't make sense. The women all have some similarities in the looks department. Then there's the fact that they're all women." I shrug. "Aren't arsonists more likely to be male than female?"

The corner of his mouth twitches. "I thought you didn't have knowledge about fires."

"Whatever." I roll my eyes but quickly focus back on the gruesome case we're working. "The arsonist is escalating. The damage he or she is causing isn't enough, stabbing the victim before setting the house on fire is different than what happened the other times. Either he or she has rage building up or merely starting a fire isn't enough anymore. Hell, it could be both."

"That's why we were called in." Arrow carefully walks through the room and I keep my eyes open while I follow his moves.

I stay quiet for the rest of our time and even during our ride back to his house. All while my mind is loud with all the things running through it. Not just about the arson case but also everything concerning Fabio.

Why can't I put my rambling mind on hold? The only moment it hit pause was when Arrow gave me what I asked for. He swooped me off my feet by worshiping my body and mind along with it.

We enter the house and Arrow stalks straight to the table to thumb through the file. I wring my hands and think of a way to ask for another favor. He gave it to me once under pressing circumstances.

"Out with it, Ginny. You've been brooding for over an hour now. Just tell me what's bugging you," he rumbles without looking up.

I bite my lip and close my eyes in an effort to think how I should ask him if he wants to have sex.

"Ginny." My name is voiced so close to me, I can feel his breath feathering over my lips.

I yelp and take a step back to stare at him with wide eyes. He takes a step forward and my breath hitches. Taking another one back, he yet again closes the distance.

"Ginny," he grits. "Quit playing around and tell me what the fuck is going through your mind."

"But what if I want to play?" I whisper.

Now his breath catches and he swallows hard. One of his hands grips my hip, the other cups the side of my face. "Don't get my hopes up if you're not sure."

"I am sure. Our circumstances the first time might have been fucked-up, but I don't regret a single second of our time spent."

"Thank fuck," he breathes out in a pained voice. "Because I've felt damn guilty for everything feeling so damn good when I was inside you."

I lean into his touch.

He connects our foreheads and murmurs, "Once I'm in, I won't be able to walk away this time. Fucked-up circumstances aside the last time, this right here is us. There's freedom in our choice to move on from here on out. I choose you. Today, to-morrow, and every day from here on out 'cause you haven't left my damn mind since the moment I saw you."

I place my hands on his chest and fist the leather of his cut. "You let me choose you at my darkest mo-ment; when I wasn't given a choice. You made me feel. Treasured, above everything else, in a world of hatred and ugliness you swooped in and let me prove to myself I wasn't lost."

"You were never lost when your soul shines so fucking bright, it's a beacon for mine to guide you home," he croaks and slams his mouth over mine.

His lips move over mine, tongue seeking entrance to sweep in to taste me. There are a lot of things I'll never understand, and the magical reaction of my body to his is one of them. Instant fire licks my veins and causes warmth to spread in my chest while the place between my legs starts to tingle and throb.

His hands start to roam and I moan in appreciation when his fingers slip under my shirt. There are no negative experiences to sex clinging to me, not when I'm wrapped in Arrow's scent. The way his familiar hands cherish my skin, his soft murmurs, his lips, all familiar and safe.

Now if he was to shove me to my knees, force me to keep my eyes open as he shoves his cock into my mouth? Things would be very different. The main reason why I've also cut off all my hair is to prevent people from gripping it, so luckily that trigger is gone as well.

I let myself sink into the pleasure he gives me and forget everything else in this fucked-up world. Even if it's for a fleeting moment in time.

CHAPTER FIVE

ARROW

I want to fucking devour her. Dig my fingers into her skin, mark her as mine in the most primal of ways by shoving my cock deep inside her. Piston in and out until I'm ready to blow and then grab my length to shoot the cum all over her pussy and lower belly. Rub it all into her skin to cover her with my cum, brand her, and make sure she smells like me.

I pull back and place my forehead against her shoulder to take a shuddering breath. My thoughts are too vivid and I'm too damn scared to fuck this up. Meeting her under dark circumstances, colliding, thrown into havoc, both gaining scars, then ripped

apart and thrown back together. One, some, all…
it tells me that this woman is meant to be mine.

"I need you, Arrow," she whispers.

Her request is loud and clear and feels as if she's
throwing a warm blanket over my shivering soul. I
keep my eyes open and locked on hers. The desperation is vivid on the surface, both needing to soothe
the ache for one another that's rooted in our veins.

My body kicks into gear and I easily swoop her
up and head for my bedroom. Placing her on her feet
before the bed, I slowly peel off her clothes. All while
her eyes never leave my face. It's as if she needs to
assure herself who's here with her.

We haven't discussed in detail what went on during the time she was taken. Though, the open-mouth
gag found when her house was breached leaves
nothing to the imagination. This right here between
us, the setting, the feelings between us are of our
own desire. No obligation, no obstructions, fucking
nothing except for the lust that's there for the taking.

I shrug out of my leather cut and throw it on the
desk in the corner. My shirt is next. The clink of my

belt, the zipper, and a quick shove down while I work on my boots, leave me completely naked.

My mouth runs dry when I catch her hand sliding between her legs, finger teasing that bundle of nerves right above her slit. It comes to a complete stop when I fist my cock and give it a rough tug.

"That's new," I hear her croak as she brings herself up on her elbow.

The corner of my mouth twitches when I flick my piercing. "Reverse Prince Albert." There's a bent barbell puncturing the urethra from the top of my shaft and straight through to the opening. "I've heard it's stimulating for both partners, but I've yet to experience it. After everything that happened, recovering from my injuries, not being able to see or be near you, I thought I might as well have my cock out of commission."

Her smile is blinding when she says, "I've never seen a pierced dick."

I chuckle and can't help but tell her, "You'll be getting acquainted with one very fucking soon."

She licks her lips and whispers, "Yes," as she lets

her legs fall open.

Swallowing hard, I place one knee on the bed and inch closer to look at her pink, glistening pussy. There's a tiny strip of hair neatly trimmed on her mound. Palming my cock, I let the head slowly tap her bundle of nerves.

A gasp leaves her as I ask, "We've had this discussion a few months back. I'm still clean, no one else since I've had you."

"They never touched my pussy and I've had a full checkup two months ago. Birth control shot. I have to schedule a new appointment soon to ensure effectiveness. I should probably tell you that...I can't...it's–"

I place a hand on her thigh. "We're both naked as the day we were thrown into this world, both endured shit, both came out stronger and found one another again. There's nothing you can't share that'll send me running, Ginny."

"I don't think I'll ever be able to give you a blow job," she blurts.

Her hands flash up to head for her face but then

she slams them down on the mattress beside her and grips the sheets. Eyes pin me in place and it's as if she's decided to scrutinize my reaction rather than hide from embarrassment and shame. And I see those two specific things in her eyes and the faint blush tainting her cheeks.

"Darlin'." My voice is firm while the look I give her is soft and understanding. "Anyone who would put demands, sexual expectations, and their own pleasure before a relationship is an asshole who doesn't respect his woman. I'd never expect you to suck my cock, but I can tell you I'm dying to get a taste of your pussy. Though, if any time during our intimacy you're overwhelmed you're allowed to hit the brakes. Understood? No fucking pressure whatsoever. If you'd want to wait to have sex another month, or a year…time is lacking when it comes to healing the scars of your mind. I'd be grateful to have you in my arms, in my bed, and simply hold you as we spend time together for as long as life allows."

Unshed tears fill her eyes and I want to lighten

the mood, so I shrug and tell her, "But any time you want to experiment to push your limits…my dick is all yours."

The smile is back on her face and a spark of mischief drives away the unshed tears.

"All mine to experiment with, huh?" she teases and her gaze lands on my dick, making it twitch.

"All yours," I agree.

And it's the motherfucking truth 'cause the sight before me where she's naked and all laid out in front of me takes my damn breath away. There isn't another woman alive who captures my attention or comes close to who she is. Ginny is my kind of perfection who merges with my flaws and mirrors my scars.

I move down her body and hold her gaze as I lean in and slowly trail my tongue through the lips of her pussy. Her taste explodes in my mouth, and I close my eyes to groan and savor the moment.

Damn. I should have devoured her pussy the first time we were together, but due to the circumstances, we basically skipped over it and immediately jumped one another's bones. Now, though? We have all the time in the world and I'm not leaving this bed until I get my fill.

I use my thumbs to spread her open. She gasps and groans, enjoying what I give her. Her gaze is heated and she props herself on her elbows to stare at the sight before her. I'm pumping two fingers inside her slick, tight pussy.

Flicking her clit, I get some more moans, and by the way she's biting her lip, I can tell she needs more. The first time we shared had elements we both needed to make our cover real and yet I know damn sure it's something deep Ginny and I share. Testing my theory, I take the little bundle of nerves between my teeth and put pressure on it.

"Yessss," she whispers. "More."

Fucking knew it. A flood of wetness trickles out of her pussy. We both enjoy a bite of pain with our pleasure and it's exactly what I gave her the first time we were intimate. Only then she needed the marks to make it real for those who held her captive.

It's also one of the things I have been struggling with and why I subconsciously must have pushed her out of my life when I woke up from the medically induced coma. Guilt is a fucking bitch and it's weighed heavy on my chest.

Not anymore. I drag my fingers out of her tight heat and glide them right back inside, curling them at an angle she likes. Instead of focusing on her clit, this time I turn my head and sink my teeth into the soft flesh of her inner thigh.

She screams out in pleasure and I feel the walls of her pussy strangle my fingers. I growl and pump a few more times before pulling out and diving my tongue right into her. Licking her clean, I let her come down from the pleasure I gave her. Climbing up her body, she turns her head and I'm not liking the way she denies me her eyes.

"Look at me," I snap, probably a little too rough.

She completely freezes underneath me until her breathing starts to pick up and not in the desire kind of way, but due to what I'm guessing is a fucking panic attack.

"Ginny," I start but then she's pushing against my chest.

She's damn strong and catches me off guard when she bucks her hips and jolts from the bed.

"You don't get to tell me to fucking look at you," she snarls. "I don't have to look at you. I can fucking look or close my eyes. You don't own me. I do. Me. Not you. ME!"

Her chest is heaving and she's waving her hands to add strength to her words. Eyes wide and face a mask of fury. There is no reason for her outburst and a gut feeling tells me this is tied to the shit she had to endure.

I hold up my hands, palms up, and stay on the bed when I gently tell her, "Your decisions are always yours, sweetheart. If you don't want to look at me then don't. All I ask is that you don't hide from me. Not ever. You can call me every damn name in the book or stand there and give me hell, but at the end of it? We will come together and each time we'll come out stronger."

She stares at me and I watch how her shoulders go down, her head drops and she covers her face with her hands. Sobs slip through her fingers and she spins around to dash into the bathroom.

Yeah, fuck that. I should respect her privacy and all, but she's teetering on raw feelings and I need her to know it's normal and that I'm right here for her. She's not alone. And if I let her lock herself away? That's exactly how she'll feel.

My hand slams against the door to keep it from knocking me in the face so she can close and lock it. She gasps and steps back. I don't give her a chance to retreat, curse me, or do anything other than sag against my body as I pull her against me.

Ginny stiffens and then starts to thrash so I hold her tighter and tell her in a soothing voice, "Let me hold you, darlin'. Please let me fucking hold you. It's killing me to see the turmoil you're in and I hate it even more that I was the cause of it."

She freezes in my embrace, except this time her head comes up, knocking me right in the damn chin. Fuck. Tears spring in my eyes and she manages to get out of my arms. Instead of walking away she reaches for my face and rubs her thumb over my chin while rubbing her other hand over the top of her head.

"I'm sorry," she croaks.

I blink a few times and clear my throat. "There's no reason to be sorry."

She shakes her head in denial. "It's not you. You weren't the cause of what just happened, and I am sorry for head-butting you."

I can't help but snicker. "Okay, you did head-butt me there. Also, not exactly your fault, though, with the both of us in close proximity of one another."

This time she comes to me by her own choice and snuggles close when I wrap my arms around her. I bury my nose into her short hair and breathe her in. We're completely naked, our bodies flush against one another, but there's nothing sexual about it.

"He forced me to keep my eyes open," she whispers. "Always barked the command 'look at me.'"

"Fuck," I mutter, 'cause that's the exact same thing I snapped at her.

"You didn't know…and…I didn't know it would…I…shit."

I rub my chin against the top of her head. "It's a trigger. Something like the hair pulling. That's why you've cut it short, right?"

"Right," she grumbles with a load of defeat in her voice.

"Noted," I simply tell her. "If you think of anything else or we run into other triggers, we'll work through or around them, okay?"

"Maybe we shouldn't...maybe I'm not ready... maybe...maybe I'm just twisted. I mean...it's not normal to crave pain with...it's...shit." She tries to get away again, but I don't let her.

"Not just you, darlin'. I crave it too." I take her face in my hands and gently caress her cheeks with my thumbs. "Not every human being is created like another and it's a good thing too. Some tip the crazy scale while others just want to explore whatever that scale is made of. So to say cause options are weighed as well as choices. Now. What we did our first time blew my damn mind. Seeing you come undone just now? Fucking sexy and I enjoyed giving you that orgasm. You letting me sink my teeth into you? Marking you as mine? Sweetheart, that gets me rock-hard. Balance. We have it."

I slowly lean in to give her an out, but she closes the distance between our mouths when she rises on her tiptoes and softly merges her lips with mine. I can taste the salt from her tears, letting me become aware of the turmoil of life. Feelings are unexplainable, run deep, and can override your brain in the blink of an eye.

"Arrow." She moans and doesn't take her mouth from mine when she mumbles, "Can we please continue what we were doing before my meltdown?"

I chuckle softly and take her fine ass into my hands as I hoist her up. She wraps her legs around my waist, allowing my cock to grind against her bare pussy. Fuck. She feels good. My breath hitches and I walk us back to the bed.

Putting her back on her feet, I grab her hips and whirl her around. My hand comes down hard on her ass. Once. Twice. Three times and I have her gasping and moaning at the same time. Leaving her standing there alone just as quickly, I round the bed and plunk my ass down. My back is against the headboard and I spread my legs a little to make myself comfortable.

Palming my cock, I lazily start to tug and stare at her. Flushed cheeks, eyes filled with lust and desire as she takes me in. She's so damn gorgeous in her naked glory with open lust radiating from her.

I flick the barbell decorating the head of my cock and tell her, "Whenever you're ready, darlin'. Put that sweet pussy above me and sink down. Ride me hard so we'll both get off. Fuck. I'm dying to feel your snug heat around me."

She sucks her bottom lip between her teeth and crawls over the bed to get to me. I keep my fist wrapped around my cock to let it stay upright as she straddles me. Pussy hovering over me and I stare, mesmerized as her pussy parts and starts to suck me inside.

"Fuuuuuuucccck," I hiss through my teeth as she sinks down to make our pelvises kiss.

My fingers dig into her lush hips and I help her up and slam her back down, simultaneously surging my hips off the bed. Her nails dig into my shoulders as she cries out. Pain. Pleasure. It all spikes and mixes as we fuck raw and unhinged.

Both of us are rushing for release, needing the angle of a fierce grip. Nails digging into skin, the slapping of our bodies, moans spilling, sweat dripping, it's all-consuming. Her head falls into the crook of my neck and she bites down hard.

Sucking skin as she marks me the way my grip is bruising her hips. It's raw fucking, branding, more than bodies uniting and having sex. We run on the adrenaline rush that spikes with pleasure and pain.

I'm balancing on the edge of orgasm when I feel her pussy clench around me. An iron fist squeezing as a plea for cum. And I do fucking come. I groan as I feel the first spurts ripping from me. I slam her down and grind into her, filling her womb.

For a fragment of a second, I'm regretting the fact that it can't take root inside her. The primal urge to fill her with my child, bind her to me by creating a life together has a whole new appeal. I want it. I fucking need it. The mere thought rips an orgasm anchor from me and I shudder from the draining experience.

Damn. The first time we were together was mind-blowing. To be honest? I might have hyped it up inside my mind but this? Fuck. This? It was so much better than the first time. Damn. I can't wait to have her again. My cock twitches at the thought and it didn't even go soft.

The way Ginny sags against me and goes limp? Yeah, I completely drained her. I close my eyes and simply hold her because it feels damn good to have her there. This feels like a victory for both of us.

Not just a huge step forward in the relationship between us, but also for the turmoil inside Ginny's head. Clearly, she's still struggling, but from the outside, she's tough as nails. Soft and hard, the perfect combination if you ask me.

Her temper, sharp mouth, brilliant brain, unique looks, and fine body. Scars hidden or in plain sight, it's the complete package that draws me in. Perfection is something no one can describe or pinpoint; it's an illusion that's sold short on any level.

One thing is for sure, though. Ginerva Romy Ellis is my kind of perfection. One that comes with stone-cold realism of flaws and limitations. Yet, we're the ones setting and breaking limitations.

Living is always a messy reality where every day can feel like a sink or swim situation. At least we're together now to lean on the other one's strength and diminish the weak moments.

CHAPTER SIX

GINNY

The murmur of voices pulls me from my sleep. I raise my arms above my head and stretch while releasing a yawn. My body feels deliciously sore. A smile automatically slides across my face with the reminder of what we did last night.

Especially when Arrow woke me up in the middle of the night with his mouth between my legs. It's as if he can't get enough of me. He knows exactly what I need without asking and gives it to me in spades.

I hop out of bed and wander into the bathroom. I catch my reflection in the mirror and notice the bite marks and hickeys littering my neck, shoulders, and breasts. I should feel embarrassed and ashamed for the things my body craves, but luckily Arrow enjoys and desires the exact same thing.

I quickly handle my business and grab some clean clothes from my bag. The voices I heard earlier are coming from the kitchen. I follow the scent of fresh coffee and recognize Kessie's voice, along with Ganza, her old man.

Rounding the corner I hear Arrow grumble, "I have to wake her up 'cause she'd want to see this."

"See what?" I question.

All eyes hit me and I now notice Stephan standing near the coffee machine. Arrow holds out his hand and my feet move without so much as a single thought. He pulls me into his lap and it actually makes me feel content instead of weird, with his friends also being in the room.

"Kessie here found something interesting," Arrow quips.

I swing my head toward Kessie. From what she told me about herself, and from what the other old ladies told me, she's brilliant when it comes to computers. She used to be the contact person between the government and Broken Deeds.

Kessie turns the laptop to face me. It's a video on pause and it looks like it was taken from a security cam that's focused on a street. A dark street so I'm guessing it's nighttime.

"Okay, so," Kessie starts. "The video evidence the bar owner turned in, which happens to give Fabio an alibi during the times you said he was with you."

I grind my teeth, hating the fact that she uses the words "during the times you said" as if she doesn't believe me.

"Well, then I'd like to know why a dude who looks exactly like Fabio is driving Oscar Donkers' truck. He leaves from the alley beside the bar and arrives back close to two hours later." Kessie shoots me a grin and starts the video to show me. "Oscar Donkers is the bar owner. He's the one, right next to Fabio's brother, confirming he was at the bar."

I blink a few times as I process her words and

I'm almost too afraid to ask, but do it anyway, "Are you saying you caught them on a lie?"

She bobs her head. "Sure did. I also can't believe the detective looking in on this issue didn't check other security cameras in the area to see if their alibi checks out. Though, I'm guessing with Fabio being a cop? They simply took him at his word since he has a spotless record."

Kessie turns the laptop and starts to type away and murmurs, "Fabio does have a spotless record. Can't find anything other than…huh."

"What?" Arrow asks.

Ganza leans in and reads along over Kessie's shoulder. "He was married. His wife died on the job."

"Hit and run," Kessie says, taking over from her old man. "She was also a cop and stopped a car alongside the road. The truck that hit her didn't even stop, case was never solved. Happened six months ago."

"Makes sense," I murmur, earning all eyes to land on me.

My face heats and I glance down at my lap. Shit. How embarrassing. I've never told anyone anything about the things I had to endure. At least not in graphic detail.

"Mind sharing what makes sense?" Ganza questions.

I turn my face into Arrow's chest and let his scent fill my lungs. Last night we became close on so many levels and it gives me the strength to know I can tell Arrow anything without any form of judgment from him.

"Can we have some privacy?" I feel the request rumble through Arrow's chest.

I pull away from him and glance at Ganza, Kessie, and Stephan. "No, please stay."

Taking a shuddering breath, I try to prepare myself for sharing some of the stuff Fabio spewed at me.

Arrow gently squeezes my hip. "Are you sure? No one will judge or look at you any differently if you keep shit to yourself or only decide to share with one of us. Hell, I'm sure Kessie or any of the old ladies will be there if you feel more comfortable explaining to them."

Shaking my head, I let him know, "I'm sure because I trust every single person in your brotherhood."

He smiles down at me and I can feel my heart squeeze just by the look in his eyes.

I take a deep breath and let my eyes land on Kessie. "Fabio talked when he…when he did his thing. I tried to block everything out, but he had ways to keep my eyes open and my focus on him. The things he said…mostly name calling and other nasty shit… it was…or felt like he was punishing me. Acting like I was someone else? I don't know. Nothing made sense at the time, but the things I had to endure were all traumatic. The way I was rescued and how it ended was liberating and made me feel it was all over. Those first few days, with all your help, I didn't have to worry about anything. Then I gave my statement and my part was done. Until I discovered who exactly the man was who did those things to me and how he was still out there…a police officer…in my own freaking town."

My fingers curl into fists when I'm reminded of the fact that going to the police station didn't do shit.

"Why did it feel like he was punishing you?" Kessie questions.

"Some of the things he threw at me like, 'Take it. Take it the way you let every other cop's cock come in your dirty mouth.' And 'cheating cunt, you like being on your knees and sucking a cop's cock, don't you?'" I cover Arrow's hand where he's holding my hip and continue. "But he would also say things like, 'Did you really think you can get away with it, you dirty whore?'"

"Sounds to me like he caught his wife cheating on him," Stephan remarks.

I turn my head in his direction. "Yes. At the time I thought he hated cops because the one who kidnapped me said I was a special order. The biker wanted a female cop at his disposal."

"I think we should look into the accident involving that fucker's wife," Arrow rumbles.

I can feel my eyes widen and blurt not so much a

question, but more of a statement, "You think he has something to do with that too."

Arrow nods. "If he relived the acts of his wife on you then I sure as fuck think so."

"I'll also check for other accidents involving female cops or incidents, deaths or whatever. He clearly didn't want to draw attention to himself and yet there are a lot of factors surrounding him," Kessie says as she types away on her laptop. "Maybe that's why he searched for someone to kidnap him a female cop. Yes, we need to check all of this."

"You do that," Arrow agrees. "I'm going to pay Oscar Donkers a little visit. Mind texting me the address of his home and the bar?"

"I'll go with you." I stare at Arrow and hope he doesn't expect me to stay here or leave everything up to him now that we had sex.

"I'll come with you two," Stephan quips.

Arrow rises from his chair and takes me with him. I'm still staring at him while processing the fact that he doesn't order me to stay out of it or stay home for that matter. He grins at me as if he can hear my train of thought.

"Why don't you get some coffee while I get changed?" He doesn't leave any room for a reply when he stalks out of the kitchen.

Kessie slams her laptop closed and connects her gaze with mine. "I'm gonna head to the clubhouse and find Bee. She can help me go through every database and stuff to save time. My old man will try and find some more footage of the truck leaving at the times Fabio was abusing you. Hopefully, we'll manage to get a nice full-blown face shot from a traffic cam or something."

Ganza grins. "Fuck, yeah. You head to the club-house, I'll swing by the house to grab some stuff and meet you there."

He gives Kessie a hard kiss and jogs out the door.

Kessie is still staring after him and mutters, "I love his butt," and strolls out the door.

"I don't think I'll ever understand women until I get one of my own." Stephan chuckles.

I shoot him a sheepish look as I grab the coffee jar. "Probably not even then."

Stephan draws a chair back from the table and barks out a laugh. "You're right. But then I hopefully have you to ask for advice." He jerks his chin in the direction Arrow left the room. "You two finally hooked up?"

I take a sip of my coffee and sink down on a chair across from him. His question strikes me as odd, but on the other hand, I know how tight these guys are and always have one another's back no matter what.

Deciding to go with the hard truth, I tell him, "If you're asking if we had sex then the answer is yes."

"Good. With the shit you two went through a lot of us were unsure how things would go. I'm glad to hear those fuckers didn't fuck up your shot at happiness. The way my brother's face lights up when you walk into the room is all telling. I've seen it on the faces of couples from the first generation and every single brother of the second generation when they found their one and only. It's admirable. Also…the way you fought for him. I heard some of the things here and there, you being naked and not caring, demanding to stay by his side when he was fighting for his life. A deep connection is rare. You feel it in your gut and only know what the one and only true person is who belongs by your side when you finally meet him or her." He throws a glance over his shoulder to check if anyone is there before he lowers his voice and tells me, "I'm saving myself for the right one but now I'm thinking it might be a bad decision. I mean…what if she's experienced and I'm all fumbling and standing there with my dick in hand?"

I blink once. Twice. A few times more as I'm still trying to process this oversharing moment with the male virgin sitting across from me.

"Dude," Arrow grunts from the doorway. "I leave you alone with my old lady for a handful of minutes and you're asking her for some sex advice? What the actual fuck? And just so you know? I wasn't a virgin when I met my one and only and still stood there with my dick in hand."

Stephan's cheeks flame and I hate Arrow for walking in and spewing his opinion, yet it's also perfect. More than perfect because the things he mentioned are related to me. My heart swells because he called me his old lady.

Helping Stephan out, I bob my head and lean over the table a bit to fake whisper, "It's true. He stood there fumbling…dick in hand…as if he didn't know what to do." I glance at Arrow and add, "Even if our first time was a far cry from a date or hookup or whatever…it still was our moment."

"Damn right," Arrow grunts. "Our moment, our fucking decision."

He closes the distance and takes my face in hand before giving me a hard kiss. I grab hold of his leather cut and sink into him. My whole body lights up from the way his lips move over mine, tongue swooping in to dominate my mouth the way I absolutely adore it.

"Yeah, I definitely hope to find that kind of scorching connection." Stephan chuckles. "I'll be outside, getting my bike, and waiting on you to disconnect so we can work on the case."

Now I'm the one with flaming cheeks. Pulling back, I pat Arrow's chest. "Let's go. Plenty of time to do…whatever…later."

"Damn right," Arrow tells me once again and drags me from the chair to head for his bike.

I love being on the back of his bike. Our time together last night strengthened our connection and bond. The way he reaches back during the ride and gives my thigh a little squeeze before returning to the handlebar makes my heart flutter.

Being plastered against his back, my arms wrapped around him, hands inches from his crotch… it's more than an intimate connection. It's a promise, an understanding, a solid bond. Give and take the way he holds up his hand over his shoulder as he's parked his bike. Giving me the option to slide my palm over his, accepting his help to dismount.

Arrow jerks his chin in the direction of the bar. "It's open for business." Glancing around the parking lot where only Oscar's truck is parked, he adds, "Doesn't look like it's busy."

We stroll into the bar and indeed, it's not busy at all. There are only three men sitting at the bar. Oscar is behind it, cleaning glasses and nods as we walk closer.

"What can I get you?" Oscar asks when Stephan takes a seat on one of the barstools.

"Some answers," Stephan deadpans.

The man places his hands on the bar. "What are you bunch? Cops? Let me see some ID."

Arrow snorts. "If I had an ID I'd be shoving it up your ass. You have two choices. Either you give us answers or we're shutting this bar down. And believe me, I'd enjoy option two 'cause that would mean I get to go nuts on the interior."

I keep my lips sealed.

Stephan slides off his stool. "Gonna take a piss. Don't start kicking shit till I'm back."

Oscar's eyes widen and he focuses on Arrow. "What kind of answers?"

"Fabio Kylen and his brother Helmer." Arrow points at a camera somewhat hidden on the wall behind the bar. "You gave the cops the feed of your camera while you damn well knew Fabio wasn't in the angle."

The man nods, but says, "No I didn't know about the angle. He was here for a few hours and then

Fabio and Helmer left."

Nodding while voicing no, the man is lying for sure and it's why I growl, "You're lying."

Oscar completely ignores me. "Look, I already gave my statement and as you said, the cops have the feed of the camera. There's nothing else I can do."

"You can start by telling the truth," I remind him once a-fucking-gain.

Oscar still ignores me when Stephan comes back.

Stephan doesn't take a seat and instead speaks to Arrow, "If this fucker isn't a fountain of information we'll check out the other lead."

Stephan slightly jerks his chin in the direction of the exit.

Arrow shrugs. "Fine with me. Why don't we get some food first."

I have a feeling Stephan found out something because he wants us out of here.

"Great, I'm famished," I tell them and stalk out the door, knowing the two men are following close behind.

I head for Arrow's bike and when I turn I notice

both Arrow and Stephan huddled together. Stephan stalks off and grabs his phone to make a call while Arrow stalks my way.

"We're going to wait for a team to get here," he tells me.

Confused I ask, "Why? What did Stephan find out by taking a piss while we were talking to Oscar?"

Arrow grins. "Stephan noticed a small screen behind the bar that kept an eye on the back entrance. Not only did that fucker not give the cops that feed, which he probably has deleted, but Stephan also noticed a truck and a vehicle next to it covered with tarp."

Still confused I wait for Arrow to expand and he doesn't disappoint when he says, "Stephan checked out what's under the tarp. It's a truck that has damage on the front of the passenger side."

"Okay," I softly murmur. "And why would that be–" My eyes widen when realization hits. "Oh. My. Gosh. Could that be the truck that was involved in the accident where Fabio's wife was killed?"

Arrow has a shit-eating grin on his face. "Come

on, let's get out of here. Stephan is going to take it from here."

He straddles the bike and offers me his hand so I can get on behind him. My heart is racing inside my chest. Maybe this is the breakthrough we need to get to Fabio. If Oscar is somehow involved, he might flip on Fabio and turn him in.

One can only hope.

CHAPTER SEVEN

Two days later

ARROW

"What do you mean they let him go? How's that possible?" Ginny gasps in outrage.

It's the same feeling coursing through my veins, but I keep it bottled up inside.

Archer crosses his arms over his chest. "We're looking into it. They've processed the truck and we're waiting on results from the lab. They've gathered some DNA and it's clear Oscar's truck was involved in something, but we still need the evidence to pull through. They have Fabio's wife's DNA on file and they will compare it."

"It's bullshit," Ginny grumbles. "I can't believe

they let Oscar go while the investigation is still ongoing. Not to mention, he kept his mouth shut about Fabio. It's Oscar's truck so how do we link Fabio to it other than it was his wife that was killed? There's nothing. Absolutely nothing except Oscar who keeps his freaking mouth shut."

"We have to be patient," Archer replies and gets an annoyed "duh" stare from my woman.

Fuck. She's gorgeous when she's pissed. Hell, she's gorgeous in my eyes no matter what.

Archer's attention slides to me. "How's the arson case going?"

"No new similar arson cases," Ginny says before I can say anything. "We managed to find out a few of the women dated a guy named Perry, no last name known. We still need to talk to one of the victims."

"We were on our way out right now," I add, feeling the need to add something.

The corner of Archer's mouth twitches as if he knows Ginny completely took over debriefing him on the case I'm working on.

Archer jerks his chin in Ginny's direction. "When

is she going to sit in your chair? You were at the shop yesterday."

A confused look slides across Ginny's face, but I know damn well what my prez is talking about.

"Soon," I grunt and then let him know how sure I am about Ginny, "Any spots available in your schedule for me?"

"Swing by the shop later today. You have a client coming in at nine, right?" he questions.

"Right." I check my watch to calculate how much time I have between now and then.

Archer grins. "I'll ink the patch before your client shows up. Where are you going to put it?"

I touch my upper arm with the tip of my fingers. "Right here."

"You're going to...seriously?" Her voice is a mere whisper and her eyes are wide with realization.

"You're my old lady, Ginny," I simply tell her.

A slow smile lights up her whole face. "Does that mean I get to have one with your name too?"

"Sure as fuck. Otherwise, we get to test your loyalty if you don't," Archer bluntly tells her.

Ginny snorts. "I'd be an idiot not to accept his claim the moment he inks my name on his skin." She holds up her hands to visualize her options. Lowering one hand she says, "Being alone." Reversing the action, she lets her hand come up. "Feeling adored and having a whole group of people feel like I'm a part of a family." She rolls her eyes. "It's not even a freaking option. I chose Arrow on any given day. Besides the way he makes me feel and how much I love to be around him, I get to help out. Feeling useful instead of being out of a job. And let me tell you something. When the rug has been yanked from under your feet and you hit ground zero hard? You also know damn well when your ass lands on something uniquely good." She points at me. "He's my kind of jackpot." She wrinkles her nose. "Except for leaving his socks on the floor and his boots wherever he steps out of them. I almost broke my neck this morning."

A bark of laughter slips from me and I pull her close to give her a hard kiss.

Pulling back, I tell her, "Not sure I can promise

the boots and socks thing."

She pats my chest and stares up at me with a load of adoration in her eyes that warms my chest.

"All right, you two. Get the fuck out of here and try to see if you can find out whomever this Perry fucker is. He might be the arsonist if he's dating those women and then turns jealous or something." He turns and stalks in the direction of his office. "See you at the shop. The both of you."

I stare down at Ginny and can't help but ask, "Where are you going to ink the patch?"

She purses her lips and I can tell she's thinking things through.

I'm almost freaking out when she stays silent, but then she surprises me by pointing at the opposite upper arm than I was a moment ago. "Right here. We might not be the same height, but when we're walking next to one another our patches will face the same way."

I cup the back of her neck. "I fucking love it," I grunt and roughly kiss the fuck out of her.

She moans into my mouth and I know I have to

end the kiss otherwise we'll end up in our room with her pussy wrapped around my cock. Right now, we need to do a load of other things. We might do things our own way, but work does come first.

I pull back and place my forehead against hers. "First, we're going to work on the arson case, then we'll grab a bite to eat and head to the shop. Then I have to ink a client, but when I'm done? We're going home and then we're gonna fuck long, hard, and thorough."

She swallows and croaks, "Sounds like a plan."

I grin and lace her fingers with mine to guide her out the door and to my bike. We've reached out to one of the arson victims and she has agreed to meet us at a diner in town. We arrive ten minutes earlier than planned.

We take a table in the back and each order a soda, agreeing to eat after we had the meeting with the woman. The woman arrives and the bandages covering her hand, arm, leg, and side of her face shows she's still recovering from the fire at her house. She declines something to eat and drink and keeps glancing around her as if she doesn't feel comfortable.

"Thanks for agreeing to meet with us," Ginny states. "But we wouldn't have minded visiting you at your house."

The woman shakes her head. "No. I don't live there anymore, and I don't want people to know where I'm staying. No offense," she quickly adds.

Questions are burning at the tip of my tongue, but I'm letting Ginny take point since the woman looks comfortable enough with her.

Besides, Ginny seems to draw the questions straight out of my mind when she asks, "Is it because you think someone you recently met started the fire?"

The woman shrugs. "Maybe. I don't know. I mean, the first time in years I agree to go out with a man, and then…the same night someone sets fire to my house."

Ginny and I share a look before focusing back on the woman. "Would you mind sharing the man's name?"

"Perry. Perry Herwins. He owns the bakery across the street. The date didn't exactly go as planned." The woman winces. "Maybe it was me being out of the dating scene for the past three years, but I wasn't comfortable with having sex on the first date. He was charming and sweet, but...no...I wasn't ready, to be honest. He was very sweet and thanked me for a lovely evening. Even gave me a kiss on the cheek and reminded me to swing by the bakery in the morning so he could give me the number of a plumber he uses since I needed one. Well, not anymore. What I mean is...he was nice and...I don't know. I don't feel comfortable accusing someone or pointing fingers...but he doesn't seem like someone who is out to hurt anyone."

"We're just checking out every possible angle," Ginny softly tells her. "I hope you don't shut out other people completely. Returning to the dating scene is always scary no matter what. Maybe you could reach out to the nearest burn recovery support group. It might be nice to find someone to talk to."

"You're not the first to suggest that," the woman

murmurs. "I might."

"Good," I rumble and the woman's eyes widen a fraction as if she just realized I'm sitting at the table too.

We spend another fifteen minutes talking and then she leaves. Ginny and I order some food and make some small talk. After sharing the same space the last few days it's surprising how easily we fall into a comfortable routine.

There are no awkward silences or forced moments. Who knows how it will be in a few weeks, months, or even years. No one can tell, but at least we're good together in the now because that's where we live.

I wipe my mouth and throw the napkin on my plate. "Want to head to the tattoo shop early? I could ink you before Archer can ink me."

She shoots me a grin. "Sure. Maybe we'll have some news from Kessie when we arrive."

"I'm sure she'll have Perry's full background by then," I agree.

"Okay, I gotta pee, and then we'll go," she tells

me and jolts up to head for the back.

I watch her ass sway and realize I like her a lot. More than a lot. Even the way she's comfortable enough to tell me she needs to pee instead of excusing herself to go to the bathroom. I lean back and take my eyes off her ass when she disappears into the hallway.

The smile on my face is huge and I pull out my phone to shoot my prez a quick message to let him know we'll be at the shop in a few minutes. I can't explain it, but I feel someone watching me and I look up from the screen to glance around the diner.

A man across the room is wearing a baseball cap that's pulled down to hide his face. Not very well 'cause I instantly recognize the fucker and shoot a whole different text to Archer before shoving my phone back into my pocket.

I get to my feet and the fucker mimics my damn moves. Fuck. It can only mean one damn thing. If this fucker is keeping an eye on me? His damn brother is targeting Ginny. Rushing forward, I head into the hallway and wait until I'm out of sight.

My heart is slamming against my rib cage while my mind is telling me to search for Ginny. Seconds seem like minutes but finally, the fucker rushes into the hallway. I'm a hundred percent sure it's Helmer Kylen and it's all I need to pull my arm back and clock the fucker against the jaw. He goes out like a damn light.

I burst into the ladies' room and shove the doors of the stall open one by one, but it's fucking empty. Spinning around, I head for the exit and come to a stop in the alley behind the diner. Across the building is a dumpster and right next to it is Fabio staring down at Ginny.

She's in the fucking dirt and Fabio has blood dripping down his chin. Fabio swings his leg back, clearly wanting to kick her. Within a few strides, I'm standing in front of him and intercept his move by shoving him backwards.

The force of my push is enough for him to stumble back and land on his ass in the dirt. I bring my arm back to offer Ginny my hand without giving her my attention. I need my eyes to stay on the threat in front of me.

"Assaulting a police officer, asshole? Not a smart move," Fabio growls. "Get the hell out of here and mind your own business. This is a police matter."

I snort and am about to say something but the back door of the diner opens and Helmer stumbles out.

Fabio spits on the ground. "Now. Like I told you–"

The rumbling of bikes interrupts Fabio and cuts off whatever the fucker was saying. Fabio takes a step forward when the rumbling stops, but I notice Wyatt jogging into the alley.

I raise my voice. "So, you were saying something about this being a police matter?"

The back door of the diner opens again and Archer along with Vachs and Rack step into the alley.

"Well, well, well. What do we have here?" Archer croons.

"A police matter apparently…according to Fabio here," I tell my prez.

"That so?" he grunts.

Fabio whips out his badge. "You bikers better step back or I will have no other choice but to arrest you."

Wyatt barks out a laugh. "Is this fucker for real?"

I feel Ginny's hand fist the back of my leather cut as she leans her head against me. Dammit. I want nothing more than to pull her into my arms. Fuck it. I reach back and circle her waist to pull her flush against my body.

Fabio narrows his eyes. "Helmer, call–"

I step forward and punch the asshole in the shoulder. "Nobody is doing anything for you. Not ever again. You're going down."

Fabio narrows his eyes and takes a step in my direction before he hisses, "I'm spotless. No one has anything on me."

I give the asshole a feral smile. "How about manslaughter? Something your wife would want at least, don't you think? But that'll be too mild for what you did to my woman."

"Bullshit," Fabio roars. "You have shit. You're not even a fucking cop. Do you think I'd let some biker scum threaten me? Think again."

"Oh, I'm thinking, okay." I chuckle. "Something along the lines of you faking to be biker scum in an effort to throw everyone off. But we're on to you, asshole."

"Okay, we're done fucking around," Archer rumbles. "Arrow, take your old lady out of here and make sure she's okay. I'll deal with this asshole here who thinks he can hit a lady, a Broken Deeds MC old lady, without consequences."

I recognize an order when I get one and I lead Ginny into the diner. I grab my wallet and make sure to throw a few bills on the table to cover our food and drinks. Ginny's head is down and I hate the defeated and hurtful look on her face.

Though I'm pretty sure it won't last long 'cause from what I know about her, she's pretty damn fast at recovering and it's then the feisty and angry attitude rears its pretty little head. Till then I hate myself for being careless.

I should have protected her better. Fabio never should have had the opportunity to come near her.

And I swear, until that fucker is dealt with I won't be leaving her side. Not now, not fucking ever.

The ride to the tattoo shop is short and when we dismount my anger has blown completely out of proportion. I can't form a single coherent word and only curl my arm around her waist to guide her into the shop.

"Motherfucker," I roar as the door falls shut behind me.

My sister rounds the counter and starts to sign. She might be deaf, but she's aware of my outburst through other things. She starts to sign and I barely manage to give her a quick update on what happened.

She shoves me against the shoulder and it's one of the rare occasions where she uses her voice when she adds, "Go."

I release a string of curses under my breath and stomp to the refrigerator to grab some ice. Grabbing a clean cloth, I stroll back to hand Hadley the stuff. She takes them from me and gently presses the covered ice to Ginny's cheek.

I grind my teeth, knowing Fabio touched her. Fucking hurt her. The need to kill him with my bare hands arises and I take a step in the direction of the door, but my sister shoves me in the shoulder and turns my body to face her as she starts to sign.

"What's happening?" I hear Ginny ask.

"Your old man here wants to track down who-ever hurt you and kill him," I hear someone state and before I know it, Ginny is in my face.

"You can't do that. He's not worth it and I don't want you in trouble because of him. He'll get what is coming soon enough. Kessie told me this morning they were on to something but couldn't explain any-thing yet. Stay. Please. Archer is handling it."

One side of her face is still red from where the fucker punched her. I reach out and feather my thumb along her cheek. My damn chest painfully constricts. Standing before her like this I know damn sure there's not a goddamned thing I can deny my woman.

"Okay, sweetheart," I croak. "Anything for you."

I hear a sound of disgust and the muttered words,

"Such a goner."

"My gag reflex is on repeat ever since we came back to town," a female says.

Both voices settle in my brain and I pull my woman close to glance over her head at Asher and Leontine, Chopper and Ivy's twins. "When did the annoying twins get back in town?"

The door of the shop opens and Archer along with the rest of our brothers stroll inside.

"Motherfucker," Archer roars.

"Is that the new way of entering the shop from now on?" Leontine quips. "'Cause I sure as fuck could get used to that."

"Right?" Asher chuckles. "So glad to be back. I feel right at home."

"Uh huh," Leontine agrees. "As if we never left."

Ignoring the annoying twins, I ask Archer, "What's wrong?"

"At the time we didn't have shit to hold Fabio or his brother for that matter, but Kessie just called. She's managed to get him on video. You'll get all the details when we get back to the clubhouse. Long story short, we let Fabio and Helmer go and they hit the road. When we walked back to our bikes they were long gone and that's when Kessie called. Now we have to haul ass to get them all while we had them mere minutes before."

Relief courses through me and I stare down at Ginny who is smiling up at me, probably thinking the same thing I am.

"Who the fuck cares," I state. "Fact is we have him. He's going down."

"As soon as we fucking find him. Him and his fucking brother 'cause he's an accessory," Archer agrees.

CHAPTER EIGHT

GINNY

My heart is racing for the second time today. The first was due to terror coursing through me. This second time, though? All the feels in a freaking good way. I'm staring at Arrow whose face is serious as he wipes my skin and dips the needle of the tattoo gun into the red ink and continues to ink me.

I shouldn't be aroused at the sight, but the fact is…I sure as hell am. After he calmed down from the turmoil we went through with Fabio, he asked if I still wanted to get inked. I could see the pain and regret in his eyes when he said it was his fault I was hurt and how he vowed to never let it happen again.

There's no way I blame him for someone else's actions. I do blame myself for letting him catch me off guard and in those few seconds of weakness Fabio was able to pull me into the alley. By then my training kicked in and managed to get a few direct punches in. I still ended up on the ground when Fabio kneed me in the ribs and knocked the wind out of me.

That's how Arrow found me. To be honest? From there on it only went up after Arrow offered me his hand to help me get to my feet. Arrow might think he failed, but in reality, he's my own personal savior.

One who is only human and can't have eyes and ears everywhere and yet he has 'cause he came after me. Saved me once again. I don't have a hero complex, maybe a little when I lust after his muscles and strength, but I respect and adore the person he is deep down.

It's the reason why I wanted him to ink the patch on my upper arm. I fully accept his claim along with the person that comes with it. There's a proud smile sliding across his face as he wipes my skin once again and leans back.

His eyes never stray from my skin when he turns off the tattoo gun and places it on the small desk beside him. "Fucking perfect," he murmurs.

"Yes," I agree and keep staring at the man who is my kind of perfect.

His gaze slowly slides up to collide with mine and the proud smile turns into a grin. Reaching out, he cups the back of my neck and pulls me into a kiss. His tongue sweeps in and glides against mine. I moan and grab his leather cut, something I love doing to pull and keep him close.

A growl rumbles into my mouth and then I'm pulled from the chair and to my feet. I gasp from the urgency of his fingers ripping at the fabric of my pants. Within a few breaths, my panties and pants hit the floor. He unbuckles his belt, unzips his jeans and pulls everything down just enough to reach for his cock.

He's tugging me to him while his other hand is fisting his hard cock. Pre-cum is already leaking from the tip as if he's set to blow any second. I lick my lips and quickly straddle him to let my pussy hover over his hard length. Arrow stares at my center as he lets the tip of his dick slide through my lips, coating himself with my juices.

"So fucking ready for me. Look at that," he croaks. "All glistening, greedy to suck me right in there."

His free hand grips my hip and he pushes me down roughly, causing me to impale myself on his cock. Pain mixed with pleasure knocks the air straight from my lungs. I've never felt more alive than within this moment.

My heart is racing, connected intimately with the only man who has rapidly become my whole world. All while he's staring up at me with open desire and adoration. I place my hands on his shoulders and slowly lean in to kiss him.

He welcomes my tongue and takes my hips in a punishing grip as he roughly helps me to bounce on and off his dick. Our kiss becomes erratic, both of us moaning, chasing the pleasure I can taste on his tongue.

"Fuck, you feel good. Gonna brand you inside out with my cum. Fuck. Yes. Come on, darlin', bounce and squeeze my cock. So. Damn. Good."

I tip my head back and gasp for my next breath. His words are like a match hitting gasoline; the spark I need to ignite an orgasm inferno. It's all-consuming, causing a scream to rip from my throat as sweet bliss takes over my body and mind.

I feel Arrow's arm wrap like a vice around my waist, holding me tight to make sure he's rooted deep as he shoots hot pulses of cum inside me. His teeth sink into my neck, biting down and grounding me with the mixture of pleasure and pain only he can give me.

Collapsing into his embrace, I try to calm my racing heart in an effort to catch my breath. Holy shit. It's as if both of us gave it all in a matter of minutes.

"Needed that," Arrow rumbles against my neck.

There's a knock on the door followed by Archer's voice. "Sounds like you're done in there. If you want me to ink your patch...I'm free now."

"Oh my freaking gosh," I whisper hiss. "We were

loud, weren't we?"

"You were loud." Arrow chuckles. "I managed to hold back...some."

"Right." I snort and snuggle against him. "Only because you bit down and muffled the sound."

His chuckle switches to a bark of laughter. "You love it when I do that."

"You too." I feel a smile slide across my face when he places a soft kiss on the spot where he bit down a moment ago.

He reaches for some tissues. "Okay, lift and I'll catch the mess."

"Do I have to?" I groan and would rather stay in his embrace.

"I'd keep you impaled on my cock and wrapped in my arms forever if I could, darlin'. Though, right now? I kinda also want to get my ink to properly claim you as mine in front of my president."

"Fine," I grumble. "If you insist."

A sexy rumble ripples through his chest when I ungracefully step away to let him slip from my body. I take the tissues and clean up before putting my panties and pants back in place.

Arrow starts cleaning his station and says, "You can head out, I'll be done in a few minutes."

"You're crazy if you think I'm going out there by myself to get hit by eyes that know we just fucked." I cross my arms in front of my chest and lean patiently against the wall.

His mouth twitches, but he's smart enough not to laugh out loud. Arrow strolls out of the room first a handful of minutes later and I follow him to Archer's station.

"Have a seat," is all Archer says.

Bee pops her head into the room and glances at me. "Hey. Austin and Jersey are here and have the information about Perry something? The arson case. Kessie was busy and handed it off to them."

I get to my feet and look at Arrow. "Are you okay if I check what they have?"

He shoots me a grin. "Let me know what they found out. I'll be right here if you need me."

Walking to him, I plant a kiss on his lips and follow Bee.

"You two are cute together. I'm happy that both of you found your way eventually. We all knew the two of you shared a connection when they brought Arrow to the hospital. I've heard what went down when the both of you got hurt. I think everyone's heart stopped for a moment right then and there." She pulls me into a hug. "My old man gave me an update about what happened today. Arrow already gave the order that you're not to be alone until that asshole is in custody. We all have your back, Ginny, the way you had ours when Arrow asked you to stay and go undercover…before you met any of us."

"Thank you," I croak and tighten my arms a fraction to relish in the warmth she gives me–both mentally and physically–through her words and embrace.

Bee pulls back and gives me a stern look. "Always, Ginny. Al-fucking-ways."

I give her a beaming smile as she points to a door in the back. "There's an apartment above the shop. Arrow's sister used to live here, but ever since she became Vachs' old lady they moved to a house located on the Broken Deeds property. Come on, we can talk privately."

I follow her up the stairs and find Austin and Jersey sitting at the table with a laptop in front of them.

"Perry Herwins is just a horny fucker who owns a bakery so he has a nice flow of women coming in," Austin rumbles as soon as I take a seat.

The corner of my mouth twitches. I've heard from Jersey that her old man is straight to the point and calls it how he sees it. Austin has a high IQ and what some might label as a photographic memory.

"So, he's connected to all the women whose houses were set on fire?" I assume.

"We went by the bakery before coming here and had a little chat with him." Jersey shoots a glance at her old man. "Well, I did 'cause grumpy here didn't want to inhale those carbs." She leans in and fake whispers, "He's on a diet."

"Am not," Austin grunts. "I just don't want to look at those fucking donuts I know they sell there."

Jersey snorts. "Like I said, diet." Her attention lands back on me when she continues, "I showed him a photograph of each of your female arson victims and he confirmed he went out with every single one of them."

"Wow. Normally that would make him a prime suspect," I mutter.

"Absolutely," Austin grunts.

Jersey bobs her head. "Normally, yes. He might be a good actor, but I got the impression he was rather shocked when I told him what happened to those women."

"I saw his expression," Austin says. "I don't think he was acting either. Legit horror washed over that man's face."

We fall silent and I don't know why the thought of Fabio enters my brain, but it somehow does. His actions were because of his wife cheating. At least, that was the motivation we came up with why she was killed by a hit and run and what he spewed when he was…I quickly shut down the dark memories entering my head.

"Maybe it's a jealous woman taking revenge on whomever Perry dates," I blurt. "I've done some reading these past few days. Aren't most female arsonists all about revenge? I think I read it in some article." I can feel my eyes widen and dig my phone from my pocket. "The scene Arrow took me to, I took a video of the people watching."

I tap the screen and search the gallery to click on the video. Placing it on the table in front of both Jersey and Austin, I point her out. "The woman with the blonde curly hair, green sweater, and thick hoops in her ears."

Bee reaches for the laptop and lets her fingers dance over the keys. "Jersey, take a screenshot of her face so I can run it."

Jersey takes my phone and within a few minutes Bee pulls up a file. "Eloise Kassina. Twenty-one, still lives with her mother...and has a part-time job at Perry's bakery."

"Well...that's a straight link," I mumble.

"She's on the top of the suspect list as of right fucking now," Austin agrees. "Want us to take over?"

I bite my bottom lip and think about his offer, but all my mind comes up with is, "This is Arrow's case. He's point on this one and right downstairs. I think it's best to ask him that question."

Austin gives me a grin and a nod. "You'll do, Ginny."

He rises from his seat and disappears from the room.

"I'd go down after him if I were you," Bee quips. "I'm pretty sure Arrow would want you there to ask your opinion."

As if on cue my phone–which is still lying on the table–vibrates with a message from Arrow.

"Told you." Bee smirks.

"I'd better go check." I grin and take the stairs down to the tattoo shop to step into Archer's room.

My eyes instantly fall on the patch that's stenciled on Arrow's shoulder. Archer has started to ink, but he's far from done.

"I heard you shoved a woman to the suspect list who might be the arsonist we're looking for." Arrow is wearing a proud grin. "Did you want us to handle it or let Austin and Jersey wrap things up?"

I would like for us to follow up on this major lead that will probably close the case and lock away the arsonist. Then again, the reminder of what happened today and Fabio still out there has to be a priority.

Austin and Jersey are not on Fabio's radar and I'd rather be there when news comes in about Fabio. Shit. Handling more than one case sucks. Then again, these guys are clearly used to it and work flawlessly as a team.

I give my attention to Archer. "It really sucks to decide and delegate stuff when you're involved in more than one case."

Archer chuckles and nods, keeping the tattoo gun in hand while he's resting his elbow on his thigh. The man keeps his mouth shut and his eyes on me. Hell, everyone's attention is on me as if I'm the one giving orders.

Jersey mentioned Austin used to have his own business solving cases–hired by Archer many times–before he became Jersey's old man. It's actually how they got together; working on a case. They had to share a hotel room, had sex, and Jersey woke up alone the next morning.

Long story short…Jersey was pregnant from that one-night encounter. Austin has issues when it comes to emotions and feelings. So, clearly, they had a bumpy start, but Austin claimed what he desired for a long time. Point is; they work well together. Hell, everyone does in this solid brotherhood.

I take a deep breath and share some of my thoughts as motivation as to how I came to my opinion. "I think it's best Austin and Jersey wrap this up. A fresh set of eyes are always a good thing when there are new leads. Besides, Jersey was at the bakery today to question Perry. And I'd rather be here when there are developments concerning Fabio. Also…I don't think it's good for the both of us to head out, especially after our run-in with Fabio."

"I can see why my mother is so taken with her," Archer says with a grin on his face. "This one might have been a rookie cop when you found her, but she's one hell of a team playing detective now."

"Old lady material," Austin grunts and smacks Arrow hard on the back. "You did good. Not as good as my old lady." He shrugs. "But still good."

"Fucker," Arrow growls. "Mine is–"

"Okay, enough, you two," Bee snaps from the doorway. "Before we end up in a dick measuring contest I'd say you two should quit while you're ahead since my old man has the biggest cock in this state."

"World, love," Archer says as he cuts off his old lady. "Biggest cock in the whole damn world."

"Whatever." Bee rolls her eyes and then points at Austin. "You, out. Jersey is waiting for you." Her finger slides through the air and lands on Archer. "You, finish your work. Arrow has a client coming in and needs to be ready by then. Now, I'm going to take Ginny here upstairs and we're gonna kill some time by watching a movie, chatting, and having some snacks. I'd say we've earned it due to the day she's had. If you need us? Don't text. We won't answer 'cause there might be tequila involved."

I bark out a laugh and blurt, "I love you."

Bee's eyes hit mine she shoots me a grin.

"Did you seriously tell my prez's old lady that you love her before you give me those three fucking words?" Arrow grumbles, but I can clearly hear the laughter in his voice.

The corner of my mouth twitches. "Mmmmaybe."

I turn around and follow Bee who is already walking toward the back of the shop. Tequila, snacks, a movie, a chat, one or all sounds perfect right about now. I've never had friends to spend time with when I had some to spare since I was always working and focusing on my career.

Being a part of Broken Deeds MC doesn't just give me the satisfaction of working on cases, being with the man I'm falling head over heels for–who am I kidding…I already stumbled and fell face-first into love with him–but I also have group of old ladies who pulled me into their midst.

And when we plant our asses on the couch and start drinking and chatting? It's exactly what I need to let the turmoil the events of today roll off my shoulders. Girl time. Fun time. Relish in the fact that this is now my life.

A life where I have a man, a partner, a brotherhood,

and a sisterhood, and am allowed to work on cases together. Hopefully the case that has left deep scars inside my mind will be brought to an end soon enough.

With Fabio in jail to pay for his crimes. But also, clarity for the family of his wife so they know who caused the death of their loved one. Justice needs to be done. For all of us involved.

CHAPTER NINE

Four weeks later

ARROW

"This is my fault," I growl. "If I didn't lose my shit and tell him I'd nail him for manslaughter concerning his wife then he wouldn't have disappeared."

I shake my head and feel the stare of every single one of my brothers that's sitting around the table.

"Nope," Wyatt rumbles. "It wouldn't have mattered 'cause the fucker knew Oscar's truck was seized for evidence concerning his wife's hit and run. He might be a stupid fucker with a twisted mind, but he sure ain't dumb. He knew there was evidence in there linking him. The perfect murder doesn't exist with technology these days, you have to be damn lucky to pull it off clean. And Fabio? Luck isn't on his side."

My VP is right but it's still a bitter pill to swallow when I realize it's been four weeks since that asshole was standing right in front of me. A handful of minutes later we had the evidence to throw his ass in a jail cell while now we're left standing empty-handed.

The evidence in question has become a large pile. The old ladies have been working on gathering everything they could find once they had the ball rolling. The truck we seized had Fabio's prints all over it, as well as Oscar's. That doesn't prove Fabio was the one driving when the truck was used in the hit and run involving Fabio's wife.

The tarp that covered up the truck, though? The only prints found there were Fabio's. Meaning that fucker was the one who covered up the truck. All substantial evidence, but like I said, there's a pile now thanks to the old ladies.

Kessie searched so far back, she managed to hack into security footage from a jewelry store across from a motel where Fabio met with the one who kidnapped Ginny. The fucker was caught on camera acting like a biker and seen entering the hotel room Ginny was brought in moments before.

We haven't showed Ginny this footage; she doesn't need to be reminded of what the fucker put her through. Due to all of this we also have full authority to bring him down no matter what. Which basically means dead or alive, but at this point I'd rather have him alive so he can rot in a cell for the rest of his life. Death would be way too mild.

"Agreed," Austin grunts. "Fucker is slippery, but we will get him in the end." He takes a file that was lying in front of him and slides it across the table toward Archer. "The arson case Jersey and I wrapped up for Arrow and his old lady is officially closed. Eloise Kassina has been transferred to a mental health facility. She basically confessed. Well, if you can call incoherent rambling a confession. Some people really have a screw loose in their head instead of a damn brain."

"What did she confess to?" Luke questions.

Louie is sitting right next to his twin and asks, "That's what I was about to ask."

"Delusional," Archer grunts as he reads from the file in front of him. "She thought Perry was completely in love with her and wanted her to take out the competition. Perry was oblivious to everything and is also seeking mental help to process all of this 'cause he feels guilty."

"Fucker shouldn't feel guilty," Asher mutters. "Can't help it if other people's insanity leaks into other folk's lives."

"Ain't that the truth," I wholeheartedly agree.

"Okay. I'm going to file this and the rest of you can work on your cases. Arrow, you're still on desk duty."

"Fuck," I grumble. "Fabio needs to be the one pulled off the streets, not me and my woman. It's been months since I've been able to work and now I've been sitting on my ass for another four weeks."

"You shouldn't complain," Austin remarks. "Your body is still recovering on the inside. It's why you didn't return to your firefighter job, right?

Couldn't pass the physical?"

"Dude," I snap. "None of your business, asshole. I didn't want to take the physical 'cause I did a lot of thinking while being away. Working those two jobs is draining and I would like some spare time to enjoy other stuff. Especially now that I have an old lady." I can't help but add under my breath, "I could pass the damn physical if I wanted to."

Austin chuckles and slaps me on the back. "Yeah, you could."

We all stroll out of church and find the old ladies huddled on the couch and surrounding chairs. Some of them get up and amble to their old man, exactly the way my woman does. A few heartbeats later and I'm pulling her into my arms.

Most of the couples leave the main room as Ginny murmurs, "Everything okay?"

I bury my nose into the crook of her neck and breathe her in. Her scent instantly calms me.

"Better now," I state.

"Yeah, well, I forgot the freaking balloons," Bee states from beside us. "My mother can swing by the store, but I really don't want her to drop by and have the kids all excited, so she doesn't leave and ends up helping me with the surprise gift bags I still need to make."

"Arrow and I can watch the kids or swing by the store," Ginny offers.

The first ten days we stayed close to the clubhouse but the weeks after we only left together. I don't want her out of my sight, but we can't stop living our lives either. Besides, we've found a nice routine where Ginny comes with me to the tattoo shop and handles the front desk scheduling clients and shit.

"That would be perfect," Bee gushes. "I'll start on the gift bags. The kids love helping me so y'all can swing by the store. Oh, and if possible…all blue balloons. It's Hunter's favorite color."

"You got it," I tell her and lace my fingers with my woman's. "We're taking one of the SUVs."

"Here," Archer grunts and throws the keys at me. "The black one is all filled up. Get some extra candy while you're at it."

"Smart man," Bee murmurs and leans in closer to Archer.

"And that's our cue to leave." I chuckle and lead my woman out the door.

"Can we swing by the drugstore? I need to get a few things," Ginny asks.

I bob my head. "Sure. What are we getting?"

She clears her throat. "Stuff."

"Stuff," I echo and glance back at my woman whose cheeks are now a bright pink.

"We're not using condoms, so we're not getting that. You haven't gotten your period since we're to-gether. You need pads or tampons and shit?"

She licks her lips and stares at her hands. "I need something else because I didn't get my period and with everything going on I forgot to schedule my birth control shot."

Understanding hits causing a huge smile to slide across my face. "Pregnancy test. Gotcha."

We're getting into the SUV when she says, "You're taking this possibility better than me."

I start the SUV and turn to face her. "You're mine.

We're living together, and have been for over a month, practically sitting on each other's lap each and every damn day. The shit you went through, adapting into what we're still going through, switching jobs, helping solve cases, and at the tattoo shop without a single complaint? You're it for me, Ginny. If the ink doesn't spell it out…I'm in this till the end of time. It's only an issue if you don't want kids." I place my hand over my heart. "Myself, I haven't thought about it till right this moment. The thought of us creating life that's growing in your belly is fucking magical and a blessing."

She's now wearing the same smile I was wearing before I got into the SUV. "Okay, then. At least that takes care of some of my nerves."

Reaching over the console, I take her hand in mine. "Some, not all. What else is bugging you?"

"I don't know," she admits. "I'm feeling on edge and have no clue why. It's as if something is about to happen, a gut feeling…I don't know."

I bring our joined hands to my mouth and place a kiss on her knuckles. "Never ignore it. Something my father used to tell me. He'd get those gut feelings sometimes when he entered a building as a firefighter. You gotta trust it and act on instinct."

"Sounds like a necessity with the risk of a firefighter. I mean…skills, experience, and training are a requirement, but I do believe following a gut feeling can make a difference."

I bob my head at her answer. "Saved my life as well as my father's on more than one occasion."

"Okay, let's be extra careful and be quick with our shopping trip. Besides, I'm fucking excited you're going to pee on a stick and can't wait to see the results." I shoot her a grin. "And just so you know? If we didn't get lucky now? I'll make it up to you and start practicing right away to try, try again…and again."

Laughter fills the air and she rips her hand from my grip to smack my chest. "You're crazy."

"Uh huh, more than a little crazy about your sexy ass, darlin'."

Twinkles dance in her eyes and I like the easy happiness radiating from her. I wasn't kidding. If she isn't pregnant, it's definitely something I'd love for our near future. For now, I have to keep my head clear and not dream away about our future.

First stop is definitely the drugstore for the pregnancy test. Then we find blue balloons for Hunter's birthday, along with some extra candy. A little over an hour later we're riding back to the clubhouse. We're almost there when I notice a car in front of us slowing down.

"What's he doing?" Ginny murmurs.

I hear a bike coming up behind us and glance in the rearview mirror while at the same time Ginny glances back. It's a fragment of a second but the gut feeling Ginny had earlier is hitting me hard.

This is the reason why I hit the brakes and grunt, "Down," as I lean in to make sure to cover her as much as I can.

The motorcycle passes us and two breaths later there's a blast that knocks out the windshield. Thank fuck I'm turned away and have Ginny mostly covered. Not to mention, if I didn't stop when I did, we would have been closer to the blast.

By the time I carefully raise my head to check if it's safe to do so, I notice some of my brothers rushing out of the clubhouse. The motorcycle is long gone and the car in front of us is nothing but fragments of scrap metal. Fuck. Body parts are all over the damn place.

Ginny wants to turn her head, but before she can do so I tell her, "Stay down, sweetheart. It's a fucked-up mess you don't want to see."

"You two okay?" Stephan asks from Ginny's side of the SUV.

I now notice the side window…hell, all windows are shattered.

"I don't want her seeing that shit," I grunt. "Call Ivy, I want her to check if she's okay. We're covered in glass. Fuck. What the hell was that?"

I might be an EMT, just like my father, but Ivy is an ER doctor.

"Don't know, but we're gonna find out," Archer says from my side of the SUV. He opens the door, glass tumbling out on the ground. "Bee is already checking the camera feed to see who was on the bike."

"Fabio," I growl as I turn to face my prez. "Had to fucking be."

"Does that mean those pieces were once Oscar or Helmer?" Ginny asks with a small voice.

I wince and curse under my breath when Ginny quickly opens the door to get out, just in time to puke her guts out on the ground.

"I'll get Ivy," Stephan says and rushes off in the direction of the clubhouse.

"Shit. She needs to lie down." I recognize my mother's voice when I'm standing next to Ginny to rub her back.

She stops heaving and spits one last time before wiping her mouth. Her eyes are closed and she sways a little on her feet.

I scoop her into my arms and tell my father who is standing next to my mother, "There's a bag in the back with a pregnancy test. Can you grab that for me and tell Ivy to meet me at my house?"

"No need to tell Ivy, 'cause I'm right here." Ivy jerks her chin in my father's direction. "Grab the test." She reaches out and gently lifts Ginny's eyelids.

"You okay, honey?"

"Sorry," Ginny murmurs. "My stomach has issues with scattered, burned, torn, and whatever body parts." She laughs without humor. "I'm still a rookie cop, I guess."

"Bury your head in your old man's chest and we'll get you out of here. If you are indeed pregnant, we'll blame it on the hormones throwing your body off-kilter." Ivy shoots her a wink.

I swear I hear Ginny mutter under her breath, "Burned flesh stinks," as she groans into my chest and wraps her hand tightly into the leather of my cut.

I glance at Archer, torn about staying at the scene to do my job, while my first concern is Ginny.

"Get your old lady settled. I'll update you when I can," he grunts.

I nod and carry Ginny out of there and onto club property. Instead of entering the clubhouse, I head for my own home. A few minutes later I have her in bed with Ivy fussing over her while I enter the kitchen to grab her a glass of water.

I know damn well she's not hurt, but my sanity

took a hit when the blast happened. Bracing myself on the counter, I take a few deep breaths to clear my mind. Goddamned. I'm normally cool as shit to do my job and not freak the fuck out.

A large hand grips my shoulder. "It's different when the one getting hurt is your woman, huh?" my father rumbles.

I hang my head. "It's like my heart…hell…everything stops until I can physically see her take a breath. Only then am I able to fill my lungs. Hell, knowing there's a small possibility that she's pregnant brings out an unknown level of protectiveness inside me. My own abilities weren't enough to check if she's okay. I asked for Ivy, dammit."

My father chuckles. "Shows there's nothing wrong with your heart or with your mind, son. Only makes it very clear you love her."

"Yeah," I croak. "I fucking do."

He shoots me a grin. "I remember when your Ma was pregnant with you. I only knew for a handful of seconds when your grandpa pulled a gun on me. Her standing behind me. Anger isn't the good word for what I felt." He chuckles. "Come to think about it…she puked right then too. She couldn't keep anything down for days and that's how they found out she was pregnant. She came to tell me and seeing her completely drained and puking her guts out? I carried her home exactly the way you did right now."

"All I needed was your father," my mother says as she strolls into the kitchen and right into my father's awaiting arms. "It was his scent that settled my stomach."

He places a kiss on the top of her head. "It's why you never left."

She softly laughs and pats his chest. "Sure it is." Her eyes land on mine. "Ginny is perfectly fine and asking for you."

I nod and take the glass of water as I head for the bedroom.

Ivy walks out and tells me, "If you need me, call. I'll leave you two to talk."

Stepping into the room, I instantly spot Ginny who is standing in front of the window that has an amazing view of the garden.

"Did your stomach settle?" I ask and offer her the glass of water when she turns to face me.

"Thanks." She clears her throat. "I brushed my teeth after Ivy cleared me. I–" Her eyes slide to the bedside table.

"You took the test," I state, spotting it right next to the lamp.

"I did." Her voice doesn't give anything away.

"I'm afraid to look," I admit. "The thought of something we created growing inside you...your body growing, belly round with our kid. Yeah. I'd like that."

She takes a few large gulps from the water before placing the glass on the bedside table. Taking the test in hand, she offers it to me.

I'm still staring into her eyes when she tells me, "I'm not looking forward to the whole body growing or pushing out something as big as a watermelon through my hooha, but...yeah."

It's then I look. Swallow hard due to the emotions clogging my throat because, "Fuck, yeah!" I bellow and throw the test on the bed to empty my hands so I can swoop her up.

I start to spin her around she grabs my shoulders and wheezes, "Stop, please stop. No spinning around."

"Shit. Sorry," I mutter and carefully place her down on her feet to gently take her head in my hands. "You make me so damn happy," I tell her and kiss her hard.

Our tongues swirl and she breathes into my mouth. Having her close, alive and healthy, is the biggest gift of all. I could have lost her today or she could have gotten badly injured. It's a hard reminder how life is fragile and it's a thin balance between life and death.

With new life growing inside my old lady's belly it's motivation enough to make sure they stay unharmed, even if I have to lay down my own life to keep them protected and safe. Though, I'm pretty damn sure this woman won't let me because she'll be right there next to me fighting whatever it is life throws at us.

I guess it's us…the way we started, collided, on

the job…still wrapped in the mess of things. It's only natural to come out stronger. At least…I fucking hope so.

CHAPTER TEN

GINNY

I place the last gift bag on the table and give Bee a grateful smile. "Thanks for asking me to help you with these. I needed the distraction."

"Me too," she murmurs and glances at Hunter and Queenie who are lying on their bellies on the carpet across from one another, each of them engrossed in a book. "Though, I'm itching to know every single detail."

"Is it always like this for you guys?" I wonder out loud. "The danger at your doorstep due to the cases you guys work on?"

Bee shrugs. "Sometimes. It's inevitable. We handle

more than one case at a time and some are complicated. It's also why we have to change things and adapt. Like the gate for instance. We've had it sabotaged, knocked down, and the last time we had prospects not keeping an eye out. We learn from mistakes, gain knowledge, and make sure to react differently."

She reaches out and pats my hand. "Your reaction is perfectly normal. It's not that my emotions have hardened over time, it's more of a hit pause moment to make sure you can push through to handle a situation. Then, when it's all set and done? We all have a breakdown moment. Even the strongest of men do. We're not made of steel, heartless, or don't have emotions. There are just qualities within that make us capable to do shit. Exactly what you were able to do when we asked for your help."

I release a deep sigh and let her words wash over me, knowing she's right.

"Besides," Bee says as her lip twitches. "Like Ivy also mentioned, let's blame the puking thing on the hormones. But I do hope it wasn't 'cause the whole morning sickness shit? Doesn't really stick to mornings. Fucking hell, I hate feeling nausea and puking? I think I'd rather have a dentist visit than puke."

"Right?" I wince.

Bee's phone starts to ring and she pulls it from her pocket. "My mother-in-law." Her eyes practically twinkle. "Wanna tell her the news?"

I chuckle and remember how Lynn had my back when she demanded Bee ask me questions during an interrogation to show I was in my right mind and could work on the case.

"Sure," I quip.

She puts it on speaker and doesn't get to say anything 'cause Lynn beats her to it. "What took you so long? Archer isn't answering his phone. Are you two working on giving me another grandchild? Is that why you two are ignoring me? Just so you know, that's the only explanation I'll accept."

Bee snorts. "I already gave you two, Lynn. But Ginny here might have some news to cheer you up."

"Shit. Arrow knocked you up already, girl?

Geez, the man works fast. I knew he only needed his dick to point in the right direction." Lynn barks out a laugh. "Another bet in the pocket. Okay, gotta go. I need to…yeah. Bye now. Oh, and Bee?"

"Lynn," Bee mutters.

"Give me another one. I squeezed out four when I was the president's old lady. It's a track record. Focus on your job. And by this I don't mean hand jobs. Those are out of the question. You already know where the cum needs to go for a homerun." Lynn chuckles and squeals, "Scoooore!"

The line goes dead and Bee stares at me with horror washing over her face.

"Did she just–" I start.

"Let's hope not," Bee whispers in shock.

"But–" I press.

"Zip it, don't jinx it," Bee squeaks. "That woman is horrible with matchmaking, predicting, and knowing shit up front. Dammit. I need to take a pregnancy test myself. I have to make sure."

A bark of laughter slips from me and Bee's lips twitch. "Shut up. I'm not ready for sleepless nights and diapers again."

She might say one thing, but her voice and face paint a completely different picture. I'd say Bee would welcome another child and the way Archer treats her and their kids? Yeah, anyone who enters their lives is treated with love and respect.

I've experienced it firsthand.

Wait. "What did she mean by another bet in the pocket?"

Now Bee is the one laughing. "I just ignore her when she gets to this point. Seriously."

I narrow my eyes. "My gut tells me you were in on this bet she mentioned."

Bee strolls to a cabinet and pulls a cookie jar from the shelf.

Handing me a chocolate chip cookie she says, "Placing bets is something Lynn organizes and can only be entered by the first generation. You know… because it involves second generation kids and their one and only."

"That little devil woman," I mutter.

Bee nods her head. "You have no idea how that

description fits like a glove sometimes."

I point the cookie in her direction. "I have another pregnancy test at Arrow's place. I bought three and I used two."

"It's also your place now," Bee points out. "You've already been living there for over the past month, the two of you have exchanged ink patches, and have a kid on the way."

I frown and again let her words wash over me. These past few weeks have flown by, while at times they were dragging without being able to completely live our lives freely. The reality is, I wouldn't change a single thing. I feel happy and right where I should be.

"Well, in that case." I grin. "I have a pregnancy test at my place you can use."

"The fuck?" Archer rumbles from the doorway, making Bee jump in place.

"It's your mother," Bee squeaks. "She freaks me the fuck out, and now I'm even doubting myself and have to be sure."

He shakes his head and closes the distance.

Cupping the side of her face, he leans in and softly murmurs something into her ear. I drag my gaze away to the one person who captures my attention any time of day.

Arrow pulls me from my chair and I feel him inhale deeply. It's as if he needs me to ground himself. I guess it's true what Bee mentioned, about them pulling through when needed, but allowing themselves to unload when possible.

Either way, the job is hard. Especially when they just had to deal with the scene of a blast where body parts were littered all over the place. The mere thought makes me nauseous again. I tighten my arms around his waist and he instantly returns the movement.

Pulling back, he tells me, "An envelope was just delivered. Ganza is tracking everything and we've already sent it off for prints. It's a letter from Oscar, taking full responsibility for killing Fabio's wife. There were even a few lines in there about him lending his truck to a friend, so it seems Fabio wasn't in his bar."

"What?" I ask in confusion. "That's not possible. Is he trying to take all the blame so Fabio is cleared?"

"Seems so," Arrow grunts.

"Won't work," Archer growls. "Fabio most likely forced Oscar to write that letter and then made him drive over here, not knowing they planted a bomb in his damn truck."

"But if Oscar takes all the blame…then there's no evidence against Fabio anymore," I mutter, mostly to myself as I think things through. "We would be back to the whole 'he said, she said,' thing we had when I went to the police station the day I recognized him."

Arrow snorts. "We're way beyond that, darlin'."

There's a load of cocky determination in his voice and I have no clue why. Does he know something I don't?

Arrow's next word explains it when he says, "We managed to track back security footage from a while back. To be specific, it's a moment where Fabio is caught on tape dressed as a biker, in front of a hotel, talking to the one who kidnapped you right before he enters the hotel room. A hotel room where moments before you were escorted inside."

My mouth turns into a silent O as I sink back down onto my chair.

I glance at Arrow who winces. "Sorry. I didn't want to bring it up to remind you of what happened. Especially since it didn't matter with the load of other evidence we had against the fucker. But just know there's no way Fabio can twist and turn to ever get out of the hole he dug himself into."

"That's…" I think of a way to put my rambling thoughts into words, but all I can come up with is, "Comforting to know."

"Yeah," Bee grumbles. "But to make shit completely comfortable we need to take him out. Him and his brother because I'm fairly sure that's the one who built the bomb. Wasn't he in the army for a hot minute until he was medically discharged after an accident? Their father used to be an explosives expert. It was in the background check if I remember correctly."

"Their father passed away last year. There's no

mention of explosive expertise in Helmer's military background. Nor in Fabio's for that matter." Archer recites facts I've also read in the background check Bee just mentioned. "We've been keeping a close eye on the house owned by Fabio and his brother. The bar as well as Oscar's apartment above along with it. Neither has returned to their homes and the bar has been closed. We have no clue where they're hiding out, but it's clear they haven't left town yet."

"Where's my laptop?" Bee mumbles to herself and stands to walk into the living room.

The kids both glance up and grin at their mother as she passes them.

When Bee returns to the kitchen she says, "I think I read something about their father moving in next door with his neighbor."

Archer moves to stand behind his old lady. We wait patiently as she fires up the laptop and makes her fingers dance over the keyboard.

"Here we go," she mutters. "A few days after his wife died, a little over eight years ago, he moved in with his next-door neighbor. The woman is still alive.

Maybe they are staying with her. Have we checked this?"

"Fuck," Archer grunts at the same time Arrow releases a string of curses.

"Why didn't we think of that?" Archer asks nobody in particular as he rubs the back of his neck. "I'll have two brothers swing by to stake the place out at a safe distance."

"Good." Arrow takes my hand and pulls me to my feet. "We're going to my parents' place. Call if you know more."

I frown. "What are we going to do at your parents' place?" I wonder.

Arrow grins. "Food. My mother asked me to bring you over. Something about pancakes not only used for breakfast. I'm pretty sure I heard her mentioning fresh strawberries, so you know what I'm talking about, right?"

My stomach decides it's a good time to agree as it rumbles loudly. Arrow chuckles and I guess I don't have to waste words and simply follow him out, shooting a quick wave over my shoulder at Bee.

"Wait up," Archer quips. "I'm walking you guys out so we can swing by your place to get the pregnancy test you mentioned."

I wait outside of the house while Arrow quickly dashes in to get the test and hands it over to Archer who returns in the direction of his home. There's a warm sense of family enveloping me as soon as I set foot inside Depay and Diamond's house.

Diamond steps out of the kitchen and holds out her hand. "Come, let those two chat about the case while I take care of you."

"Take care of me?" I wonder out loud.

Diamond rolls her eyes. "I can tell you're famished. Besides, when I was pregnant with that one there all I ever wanted to do was eat."

Depay barks out a laugh. "Damn right. I remember when I returned from a long shift, house filled with the delicious scent of dinner, but once I stepped foot inside the kitchen? I swear that one was standing guard in front of the oven to protect the food. Sharing anything edible was a rarity those months."

Diamond glares at her old man. "I wasn't that

bad."

The corner of Depay's mouth twitches. "I love you, darlin'."

I softly chuckle, knowing Depay just intentionally skipped over his old lady's comment. Their interaction warms my chest. I can only hope for a relationship with this kind of dynamic after years of being together, raising kids to grown adults.

From what I've heard their lives haven't been all roses and sunshine. Depay has the scars to prove it as well. Still, when those two look at one another the love they hold radiates from them. It's admirable and I think it's a gift to be welcomed into their family, one I'll never take for granted.

My stomach rumbles loud once again. Diamond ushers me into the kitchen where I take a seat at the kitchen table. There is a lot of bitesize food on plates that all looks delicious. I'm about to reach out when there's a plate filled with Syrniki, along with what looks like freshly made strawberry jam along with it.

I moan. "You didn't have to, but I sure love you for it."

Diamond giggles. "Eat. You need your strength."

There's no way I can reply with a mouthful of Russian pancakes so I simply bob my head and enjoy the treat she made for me. I can't say it enough, but after the dark time I went through? I went straight into the light and enjoy the warmth of the change in my life that's been given me.

A little over two hours later I feel completely re-charged due to my time spent with Bee first and then with Diamond. It's also comforting to have someone who almost feels like she's partly a mom to me.

Her understanding, words of wisdom, caring, and tenderness is something that I now realize left a large gap in my life the day my mother died. Even if it's not the same, it feels amazing to have her in my corner.

The little one growing in my belly will have a large family and brotherhood welcoming him into this world. This knowledge gives me the strength and determination to shove down any concerns that would randomly pop up inside my head.

There are raised voices coming from the living

room. Diamond raises an eyebrow at me and we both stand to check out what's going on. Archer and Wyatt are standing in the living room, facing Depay and Arrow, while Stephan and Asher are near the door.

"What's going on?" Diamond asks when at the same time Bee enters the house.

"Ivy and Chopper have the baby monitor. They are going to stay behind. Kray and North are on their way to stay at the clubhouse along with their old ladies. I'm all set to—"

"You're not going anywhere," Archer snaps. "Kessie can—"

"Most certainly not," Bee growls. "Kessie and Ganza are at the clubhouse as well because it's their turn, as it is my turn to be in the SUV to be the one on scene. Don't you dare throw pregnancy at my feet while we didn't even know earlier today. I feel fucking fine and like I said, I'll be in the SUV."

Archer grits his teeth. "Fine."

Bee's attention slides to me for a fragment of a second before she focusses back on her old man.

"Ginny will be in the SUV with me. She's a certified police officer who can hold her own."

"No," Arrow growls.

"Fine," Archer grunts at the same time.

Arrow is glaring daggers at his president. I have no clue what's going on but from the scene in front of me I'd say there were some developments, and they are about to jump into action. Action Archer doesn't want Bee involved in since she is apparently as pregnant as Lynn hoped she was.

I'm moving across the room and stand next to Bee. Queen Bee for sure 'cause she has a good handle on giving orders that need to be honored. Such as the fact that being pregnant doesn't make you incapable.

"Kevlar vest." Archer sighs as he texts someone on his phone and doesn't even look up at me and Bee. "Both of you. Everyone, gear up and meet in front of the clubhouse in twenty minutes."

Arrow stalks my way while Bee whispers under her breath, "Don't let him say or do anything to make you stay home."

I snort. "As if. I'll meet you out front in twenty."

She grins. "Good girl."

"Bad influence." Arrow glares at Bee and leads me out of the house.

A prospect jogs out of the clubhouse and comes our way with a vest. He throws it at Arrow, who catches it midair, thanks him and the prospect gives him a thumbs up as he spins around and returns to where he came from.

"You're gonna wear this and stay inside the SUV with Bee no matter what." His words are a hard demand, but then he adds in a tormented tone, "Please, Ginny. For my sanity, stay safe. There have been too many missions where shit goes wrong."

"I know." I wrap my arms around his neck and pull him close. "There's no need to remind me of what happened the last time shit went wrong. Giving you mouth-to-mouth while Wyatt was doing compressions to restart your body was enough of shit going wrong to last me a damn lifetime, thank you very much."

He grimaces. "Point taken."

"Good. Then we're in agreement. Neither of us will get hurt so we can raise this little one together and have an awesome life," I tell him to hopefully lighten the mood.

A grin slides across his face. "Sounds like a promise neither of us can deny."

My breath catches when he takes my lips in a soft kiss. The tender way he licks inside and rubs his tongue against mine makes me feel precious. We might not be ready to voice our feelings, but we sure are on the same level of adoration tipping to love.

Who am I kidding? This man held my heart the way I held his the day he almost died as I furiously tried to breathe the life right back into him.

CHAPTER ELEVEN

ARROW

I glance back one last time at the unmarked black van where Bee and Ginny are sitting inside and follow Wyatt in the direction of the house. We've had two brothers keeping an eye on this place. They reported back that there were at least two people in the house, one of them being male.

They couldn't get a visual if it's Fabio or his brother, but it's definitely worth going in and checking if that fucker is staying there. We're all geared up and made three teams. The property the house is sitting on is large.

The house next door was owned by Fabio's

father, but sold when their mother died. Probably because the man moved in with his neighbor. We've made a map of the buildings sitting on the property.

One team will be going in through the front while another takes the back. There's another team that's going to focus on a barn that's located further back. Luke, Louie, Vachs, Stephan, and Asher are heading there now.

They will also be keeping a close eye on the bushes and trees near the house that separates the property from the other house. Behind it is some rough terrain and a river running close by.

My prez is on my team while Wyatt is leading his own team around back. We're staying connected through our earpiece. Bee is handling shit on location while Ganza and Kessie are keeping an open line while they're at the clubhouse.

This way Bee can delegate in regards to issues close around us, tell us where to go if someone escapes. While Ganza and Kessie can send more teams our way or let them put up a roadblock or whatever.

By doing this, we have eyes and ears in a lot of

places. It's not a hundred percent perfect, though it has worked for us many times in the past. Like the time when Kessie saved my life by ordering a helicopter to transfer me to the hospital.

We're a well-oiled team, but unexpectant shit happens all the time, especially when you least expect it. Which is why we're always on full alert and try to come prepared by working in teams. Besides the teams we also have Rack with Liah, his old lady, as our sniper team on standby.

With Fabio being a cop and dropping off the face of the earth, taking his service gun with him, he's considered armed and dangerous. It's basically a shoot on sight order. Add this to the fact the fucker used explosives earlier today...it's safe to say we're all on full alert.

Archer sticks his hand into the air and indicates with two fingers that we're moving forward. I'm flanking him when Austin grabs the battering ram and swings it back. There's wood splitting and cracking. Austin gives an extra kick and the door swings open.

He steps back as Archer and I go in, the rest of our team following close behind us. From the other side of the house comes the same noise. Wyatt's team is also entering, but our focus is going room by room to clear it.

The first room we enter is a small living room. There's a woman sitting in a chair and she glances up with thick glasses on her nose. Her eyes go wide and a little scream of terror rips from her.

"Must have issues with her hearing," Archer rumbles. "Otherwise she wouldn't be so damn surprised 'cause Austin kicking in the door makes one hell of a noise."

We leave one of our brothers with the woman and backtrack into the hallway to clear the kitchen.

Wyatt's team goes upstairs and at the same time I hear Stephan's voice. "Suspect just climbed out the window."

There's a gunshot, another one.

"Can't get a clear shot. Fucker is returning fire." Stephan's breathing picks up. "He's running off into the…fuck."

We're all running out through the back and it's dark as shit. More gunfire erupts, coming from the section with the bushes and trees. We head in that direction but it's running blind if we all go in.

"I'm right behind you," Archer snaps. "Team two, team three, stay put."

Instead of running I carefully watch each step that I take, keeping an eye on my surroundings while trying to hear for each and every snap of a damn twig. Another gunshot cracks through the air and it's further ahead of us.

This is why I pick up speed and rush forward. A flash of white catches my attention and I recognize Fabio taking aim. Even from this distance I recognize the side profile of this fucker but the shirt also makes him an easy mark. All of my brothers are wearing black and special gear.

I don't hesitate and plant my feet to take aim. The bullet leaves my gun, but before it impacts Fabio's head, the fucker manages to pull the trigger as well. Fabio's body jerks and by the way he crumbles to the ground and Archer standing next to me with his gun in hand, I know my prez also tried to take him out.

We were successful, 'cause the fucker crumbles to the ground, but we have no clue if the bullet Fabio fired hit anyone.

"Stephan!" Archer bellows, even if it's not necessary 'cause we're all wearing an earpiece.

Though, earlier his connection was cut off. Since the threat is now gone, Archer and I run forward.

Archer drops down next to Fabio and checks for a pulse. "Target is out. I repeat, target is out. I want teams in here right fucking now. Stephan is missing. Spread out and find him. He can't be far."

I reach for my flashlight and scan the thick bushes surrounding us. I hear the clattering of water when I go right. My next step is into fucking nothing and my heart leaps. Someone grabs my vest and barely keeps my other foot on the ground.

"Fucking hell, that was close," I grumble.

Archer is standing right next to me as we both stare into the ravine I just almost tumbled into. The river at the bottom is wild and dark.

Archer releases a string of curses. "Bee, get me a damn signal on Stephan. Now, dammit."

"Smart thinking," I whisper, keeping my eyes pinned on the water.

Each of us has a small microchip inserted under our skin. Might sound insane, but in our line of work it could mean the difference between life or death. Which reminds me to put in a request for Ginny's, after I've discussed it with her of course.

I expect Bee to give us Stephan's location through our earpiece, yet the line is dead silent when Archer grunts, "Understood."

Fuck. That's not good. His eyes find mine in the dark and the grim look on his face tells me all I need to know.

"No vitals?" I ask, making sure to cover my mic and keep my voice a low whisper.

Archer gives a slow shake of his head.

Motherfucker.

"I want lights down here, search teams, every-fucking-one. Make it happen," Archer rumbles. He falls silent for a heartbeat and tells Bee, "Didn't expect anything else, but I had to say it, love."

Yeah, he had to give the order, but his reaction tells me Bee had already people jumping into action.

"Arrow, I need you to circle back and give them directions. Then make sure to send Wyatt my way and take over from him, understood?"

"Understood, Prez," I grunt and turn to jog in the direction I came from.

Wyatt is already waiting for me when I almost reach the property near the house. I give him directions and also warn him to watch where the fuck he's going since I also almost fell down the ravine.

Every single brother I pass has a grim look on his face. It might not have been voiced out loud but Stephan is MIA. No vitals showing and I have no clue if they have a location. But if I have to guess? They fucking do and it's why Archer asked for his VP so they can check together before everyone else.

"You need to see this," Asher says when I'm close to the barn.

I follow him inside and instantly spot the dead body in the corner. There's a sheet draped over the upper part. Taking in the space, I also notice the long bench with equipment.

Jerking my chin in that direction I state, "That's where the bomb was made."

"Yeah," Asher grunts.

Walking to the dead body, I squat down and take the sheet from it. Helmer clearly suffered two gun-shot wounds to the chest. He's only wearing sweat-pants and boots. The coloring on his belly tells me he didn't suffer those today.

"He didn't die today," I mumble to myself.

"No?" Luke, who is now standing next to Asher, asks. "How can you tell?"

I point at the greenish blue marks on Helmer's stomach. "Decomposition. This discoloration of the right lower quadrant tells me the organs." I look up at Luke and see him frowning so I speed things up. "Bacteria in the bowels, the color indicates decom-position and that doesn't kick in fast enough if his brother killed him before we got here. So, I'm guess-ing he killed him before he killed Oscar. Hell, maybe Oscar killed Helmer and Fabio in return planned a way to use Oscar for his own good. Who knows? They're all fucking dead."

I rise to my full length and stalk out of the barn. An hour passes and I keep busy with making sure everything is handled in both the house and the barn with the body and the woman whose house they used. All while there's still no news from Stephan.

Ganza showed up in an SUV half an hour ago. In the back were Ramrod, his daughter, Jersey, and her mother, Doll. Austin went straight to his old lady and took Jersey in his arms. Ramrod and Doll both looked devastated when I saw Wyatt talk to them.

Archer arrives and takes over from Wyatt who is now stalking my way. He comes to a stop in front of me and rubs the back of his neck as he releases a heavy sigh.

"Anything I can do?" I question.

He doesn't give me his eyes and keeps staring at the dirt underneath our feet when he says, "From what we can tell Stephan was shot and probably tumbled down the ravine and into the river. His location is somewhere downstream. He doesn't show any vitals and Bee ordered a diving team to enter the river and start searching for his body. Thing is…the river is fucking wild and it will take a while to get the team ready."

"So, he's gone?" I croak.

"He's not dead till I see his fucking lifeless body," Ramrod growls beside us. "I refuse to believe it. Even if his vitals aren't there. We all know what happened with Baton and Benedict. Those twins switched lives, Baton made Benedict…he fell into the fucking sea and turned off his microchip. Something could have happened…a logical explanation."

The desperation in his voice is killing me.

I grab his shoulder and give it a firm squeeze. "I fucking hope so, brother."

Hope is all we have at this point. Though as the hours pass this too slips. We still have search teams in place, but there's little we can do to help so Archer sent some of us home. I was ordered to take both his old lady, as well as mine, back to the clubhouse.

Bee put up a fight, but Archer was firm with his order this time and I drove the both of them home.

Chopper and Ivy were both waiting on the porch when she walked to her house. There weren't any words exchanged. Hell, what is there to say? Fucking nothing, that's what.

I guide Ginny into our house and lock the door behind us. That's it. Both of us are standing there, doing nothing.

"I feel useless," Ginny whispers. "I want to do something so bad, but I don't know what."

Taking a step forward, I take her into my arms and pull her close. She sags against me. A few heartbeats later I hear a sob escape her and it also makes my own damn eyes sting. Emotions are running hard and raw through us.

The way we discussed stuff before we left for this mission was enough to be aware of bad shit happening. This, though? Losing a brother? Fuck. We balance a fine line of life and death and luckily we aren't put in a situation very often. Getting hurt? Ending up in the hospital? Months of recovery? Yeah. Hell, I've even experienced it myself recently.

Shit is fucking twisted right now. Death is final.

Going missing is devastating. Knowing his vitals aren't registered by the microchip is a solid indication of the inevitable. Yet, like Ramrod said...until there's a body and we can see with our own eyes... then we'll believe it.

Though, he wasn't up there like I was. Didn't see the river and how the water was ruthless. This is also the reason why they haven't found the body yet 'cause the microchip has a small location window, but it's still a large space to cover...especially if the body is at the bottom of a rough river.

Emotions hit me like a sledgehammer and I bury my face into the crook of her neck. She's holding me as tightly as I'm holding her. We're grounding one another while the world around us is in full blown havoc.

I take her with me to the bathroom. Turning on the water, I let it warm up as we both strip away our clothes. There isn't anything sexual about it. We need comfort, the water to wash away our tears as we let the cold drift from our bodies.

We're both mentally and physically drained.

Turning off the water, I hand her a towel and grab one for myself to dry off. It's four in the morning and we'd better get some sleep. We can't do anything at this point, but come morning I'm sure a lot of us will need the support to process all of this. As do we.

– THREE DAYS LATER –

"How long should we continue to look for his body?" Vachs questions. "I know it's a dick move to ask, but not being able to grieve or move forward is taking its toll on all of us. Either way it's devastating."

Archer's gaze stays down on the file in front of him. "I'm respecting a brother's wishes. This is not my call nor is it yours or anyone else's for that matter. We're not going to hold a funeral, not going to hold a fucking service, not doing anything other than to let Ramrod, Doll, Jersey, and Austin handle it. I've handed it over and it's their case. Respect their decision, and mine." He opens the file and takes out a few papers. "We've been handed a case this morning that requires full priority. It's exactly what we need right now to keep our minds occupied."

He hands each of us information and continues to talk about the new case, one that involves a serial killer. We all try to focus, but it's damn hard. Everyone's mind is still on the loss of Stephan.

We were hopeful in finding him due to the microchip, but later that night they lost contact completely. Now there's no way to track his body. With the river being as rough as it is, it could have easily taken Stephan's body miles and miles away from the spot where he fell in. Which is why his family, along with the brotherhood, has taken turns searching along with a special team.

Everything till now has been useless. It's why they have cut back on people working in teams 'cause search and rescue at this time isn't priority. With the information we have there's very little chance he's still alive. Meaning it's only a matter of time until his body turns up.

Twenty minutes later we wander out of church

each with a new task to focus on. The only time I feel somewhat balanced is when I get to pull my woman into my arms. Which luckily is a lot of times, like now. After I've breathed her in, I take her hand and lead her out of the clubhouse through the back and straight to our house. Once home I fill her in on the details of the new case.

"It's a good thing to move forward," Ginny softly tells me. "Archer is doing the right thing to both honor Ramrod's wishes and keep the brotherhood sharp and focused. It's one hell of a task and burden to have on your shoulders."

I bob my head and release a deep sigh.

She touches my forearm and gives me a small smile. "I scheduled an appointment for this afternoon. Would you like to come with me?"

I blink a few times and try to think of what... fuck. The baby.

"Hell, yes," I grunt. "Sorry, my mind is a scrambled mess. I should have remembered."

Ginny shrugs. "All our minds are a bit off right now which is completely understandable considering the circumstances."

"Strange how life works," I mutter. "Life, death, throwing things up and letting it come together. Joy, pain, grief, happiness…the highs and lows we ride while we stumble and fall, only to crawl back up and keep going."

She laces her fingers with mine and gently squeezes our joined hands. "That's exactly what life is all about. And if I'm being honest? I'm thankful the darkness led me to the light you shined on my life. It makes me aware of the fact that no matter how hard we get hit, we will still have each other, along with the brotherhood, to pull us through and come out stronger."

She's right. Though I wish we'd still have Stephan here with us. It's why I pull her close and hold her in my arms, thankful for what we have for nothing in life is certain.

CHAPTER TWELVE

Six months later

GINNY

I gasp and take in the luxurious hotel room. "It's gorgeous."

"There's more," Arrow says as he places our suitcases next to the couch.

Turning to face him, I'm about to ask what else he's going to surprise me with when his mother strolls out of the bedroom with her camera in hand.

"He asked if I had the time to do a maternity photoshoot. How could I not when it involves my own grandchild?" Her smile is blinding and I feel my eyes sting with unshed tears.

Damn those hormones. This whole day has been

filled with one surprise after the other. It's my birthday and I'm now thinking Arrow has been planning this for a while now. This because I've mentioned a maternity photoshoot only once when I asked about the gorgeous pictures in Diamond's house.

She's a photographer and sells some of her photographs in a gallery. It was months ago when I told Arrow she should take pictures of us and my huge belly once I was further along in the pregnancy.

"I love it," I croak and turn to Arrow to blurt, "I love you."

He chuckles softly and pulls me to him. "Love you too, darlin'."

Placing a kiss on the top of my head he steps back and says, "My mother picked out a few things for you to wear. Go with her into the bedroom and I'll grab the stuff she ordered me to bring for myself."

His mother snorts. "I told you she'd be fine if you lose everything except for the jeans. It will give a nice contrast to her naked belly."

"Jeans and his leather cut," I correct her.

Arrow's eyes meet mine and I know he gets the need for me to include Broken Deeds MC. It's a huge part of our lives through the cases we work on together, how we met in the first place, and how it's simply family. Something our child will grow up in, and be a part of, as well.

I let Diamond lead me into the bedroom and another gasp leaves me but this time it's due to the gorgeous white, lace open front maternity dress laying on the bed that's completely see through. There are a white bra and panties lying next to it.

Now this? This is something I've specifically mentioned to Arrow. I've seen something like this in a magazine and told him about it. The tears I feel stinging my eyes do slide over my cheeks this time.

"There, there," Diamond murmurs and hands me a tissue. "Don't start those waterworks or you'll have puffy red eyes and we'll have to do a load of makeup. I'm pretty sure Arrow will be pissy 'cause I know for a fact my son has more up his sleeve for you right now. Even if he's probably not wearing a shirt at the moment."

I bark out a laugh and wipe my eyes before blowing my nose. Tossing the tissue in the trash can in the corner, I give her a full-blown smile.

I get one in return and she gently presses her palm against my cheek. "Happy birthday, sweetie."

"Thank you," I croak. "I'm so thankful to have all of you in my life."

She pulls me into a hug while she whispers, "We're all thankful to have you gracing ours."

I have to bite my lip to shove down all the emotions coursing through me.

"Come on, let's get you dressed and ready to go. I think you'll find everything on the bed so if you dash into the bathroom to change, I'll go get my makeup kit and touch up some you ruined by those tears of joy." She shoots me a wink and leaves without another word.

I quickly gather the things from the bed and stroll into the bathroom. It's a large space with a bubble bath, a rain shower, and a huge mirror wall. I place the things on the counter and kick off my shoes as I strip out of my comfortable clothes and into the white lingerie and lace maternity dress.

Staring in the mirror at my reflection is somewhat of a frozen moment in time. My hair is still short and doesn't need any fussing before stepping in front of the camera. At first, I cut it all off for obvious reasons; not wanting anyone to ever grab my hair again. Though, I have to admit…I love it now.

Arrow does too and I don't seem to have a trigger anymore if he slides his fingers through it. I haven't been able to give him a blow job and he's never asked. Touching him, jerking him off while he plays with my body is something we did do.

There's never any talk about putting my mouth on him, but I can't help the hint of fear that he might long for something I can't give him. To be honest? I don't know if I can. I would like to try and yet I'm not ready.

Taking a shivering breath, I place my hands on my round belly and stare at my reflection. I'm overly thankful to stand here. Pregnant, and a load of other things my life is graced with. There's a soft knock on the door before it opens and Diamond steps into the bathroom.

"Oh wow, you're gorgeous," she whispers and places her makeup kit on the counter.

We're smiling at one another and she gives her head a little shake. "Let's get a rush on this so I can let you two enjoy one another's company. Because if I don't? I'd be a sobbing mess. I'm so freaking happy for the two of you."

I don't entirely understand her reaction, but I let her fuss with some makeup and within a few minutes she leads me back into the main room. Depay is standing near the couch with Arrow and I find it a bit odd for him to be there, but maybe he's here to pick up Diamond or whatever. He pats Arrow on his shoulder and murmurs some words too low for me to hear.

"Why don't you two stand in front of the floor-to-ceiling window? Great lighting and it gives me the room to have the both of you fully in the picture." She takes the camera in hand and places it in front of her eyes. "Yes. Perfect."

I turn my head to face Arrow.

"Hey," he murmurs. "You're fucking beautiful."

I feel my cheeks heat and let all the love I feel for him slip into my voice when I say, "You're pretty fucking beautiful yourself."

He slides the fabric of the dress to the side and places his hand protectively on my belly. "I love both of you." He lowers his voice so the words are just meant for me when he adds, "My girls."

We know it's a girl, but we haven't shared that little piece of information with anyone. The only reason we wanted to know is because we were getting into heated discussions when it came to a boy's name.

Funny because we both came up with two names for a girl. One being Stephanie, and the other Josie. Since we now know it's a girl we will be using both names, completely dissolving all heated discussions. We can't wait to welcome Stephanie Josie into the world and hold her in our arms. All in good time, though.

Diamond gives us hints and directions where she wants us and how to pose and it's a load of snaps later when she instructs Arrow to get down and place both hands on my belly as he stares up at me. Not a hardship since the man loves to have his eyes on me.

I stare down at him, feel his hand on my belly as he's now on one knee with a ring in his other hand. I suck in a hard breath and I cover my mouth with the tip of my fingers. Holy shit. My eye catches sight of the ring he's holding and tears instantly well my eyes. It's the shape of a round, golden arrow where the tip is facing the nock, and both are set with tiny diamonds.

"My gorgeous, sweet, loving, smart, Ginny. The ride we've been on till now has the potential to fuel many, many years to come. I'd love nothing more than to welcome our kid into this world as husband and wife. So, how about it, darlin'?"

That's my Arrow. Always straight to the point. I have to give him credit, though. This proposal is definitely one I'll remember for a lifetime. And I'm pretty sure a lifetime with this man wouldn't be enough.

"Yes," I whisper, reaching out to cup his cheek. "Yes, always yes. Today, tomorrow, when we're holding our kid, and each day after that…my answer will always be yes. Yes to us."

He rises to his full length as he takes my hand and slides the ring on my finger. He gently grabs the back of my neck and draws me in for a hard kiss. I let my hands travel up from his bare chest to his shoulders to hold on tight. I hear a soft sob coming from the other side of the room and then I become aware of the fact that his parents are still here with us in the room.

Arrow breaks the kiss and chuckles as he places his forehead against mine. We don't have another moment for ourselves when Diamond pushes herself between us muttering, "Move," to his son as she grabs me in a hug.

"Congratulations," she gushes and gives me a quick squeeze before stepping back and taking my hand in hers to bring it to her face to study the ring. "Oh, Depay, look."

My hand is led through the air in Depay's

direction and he leans in to nod and then faces his son. "Nice touch."

Arrow grins.

Depay turns to his wife and then to us. "Okay, we'll leave you two to it because I've heard the actual maternity shoot will continue at the clubhouse in a few days. Something about the perfect spot in the backyard and then with a full row of bikes behind it and shit. Of course, that includes other dresses instead of the bikini and lace dress version you're wearing now."

Arrow growls low in his throat, making his parents chuckle as they grab their stuff. Diamond gives me a final wave and then the door closes behind them, leaving Arrow and I alone in this fancy hotel room.

His eyes roam my body with open lust, very differently than when his parents were present. Tingles start to spread low in my belly as excitement and desire leak into my veins. My breathing picks up and I take a step in his direction.

"So. Fucking. Gorgeous," he rumbles.

He slides his arm around my waist, slowly bringing our bodies close as he turns me last minute to make my back connect with his front. His mouth is right beside my ear, his breath hot against my skin.

"I've had to think of horrible shit inside my head to keep my cock from rising. Fuck. Hardest time I've ever spent with my parents present, and pun not fucking intended."

A laugh escapes me and I wiggle my ass against his hard dick. He moans and lets his hand travel over my belly down to the valley between my legs. Now I'm the one moaning when he slides his skillful fingers into my white panties.

"I've wanted to touch you from the second you walked into the room. Stupid to ask my parents to be here with me for our special moment, but I also know you wanted to have things like this documented. I know because I see you get all teary when you watch those short little videos on your phone of other people proposing or kids asking their stepmother or stepfather and shit. You want to have it for yourself to show our kids. And yes, I'm saying more than one 'cause hopefully we will fill our house with a lot of those little ones. Seeing you round with my child is sexy as fuck, especially today." He nips the skin of my neck and I swear a micro-orgasm ripples through my pussy.

"You love it, don't you?" He lets his tongue soothe the spot he just marked. "Love it when I keep you balancing between pleasure and pain."

The devilish man strokes my clit and pinches it right after. I release a curse and squirm under his skillful hands.

"Please," I whimper, not exactly knowing what I'm begging for, but I want it…need it, more than the air filling my lungs.

He steps back and I almost cry from anger at the loss of his warmth at my back. I should have known there was no need for my pending reaction when he takes my hips in his hands and turns me around as he falls to his knees before me.

"Take two steps back and sit down in that chair," he tells me, voice dark and rough from desire and it's all aimed at me.

I glance over my shoulder and spot the loves-eat in the corner. Slowly backing up, I multitask by sliding my panties down onto the floor. I settle into the soft cushion and throw my leg over the armrest, making my old man's eyes flare.

"Is that glistening pussy all for me?" he rumbles.

I bite my lip and eagerly bob my head, wishing he'd hurry up and put his mouth on me the way he clearly wants to.

"Words, darlin'. I need the words or you won't get my tongue sliding through your sweet pussy."

Oh, come on. Why does he have to keep rambling? Use that damn tongue to communicate in another way, specifically the language my pussy can translate for me in orgasms.

Do I tell him so? Hell no. If I would the damn man would draw it out even more. So instead, I let my own hand find my clit and tip my head back to moan at the pleasure shooting through my bundle of nerves. My next breath comes out as a gasp when my hand is batted away and replaced by his mouth. Score!

I keep my head where it is and relish in the pleasure this man always manages to surround me with. With his mouth, fingers, dick, any, all…it's the man himself who tips my happiness scale.

Being pregnant changed my body. Not just the huge belly, but also my breasts, hips, legs changed. I've gained weight and yet the man has only looked at me with overflowing desire and love. This man is one in a thousand, a treasure I will never take for granted.

I moan his name when I feel my orgasm getting closer. Almost there. Almost. But then everything stops. I'm stunned and searching for words except there's no chance to voice any when his mouth is quickly replaced by the tip of his cock prodding my entrance.

"Thought you could light up without me, did you now." He chuckles. "Not happening," he states and surges forward, filling me completely.

There's a sweet burn when my pussy rapidly tries to accommodate his hard length. Where he was feverish to bury himself deep, he's now lazy in sliding in and out of me, making it hard for me to breathe through the slow-burn he's creating.

"Arrow," I whisper.

"Yeah, baby," he murmurs.

"I love you–"

He cuts me off by rumbling, "Love you too, darlin.'"

A frustrated growl leaves me and I swear I hear him softly chuckle when I tell him, "Not for long if you don't give me a damn–"

Utter bliss hits me like a tidal wave.

"Fuck, yes. That's the way I want you squeezing my cock. Perfect," he grunts and tunnels in and out of me as if he's completely losing himself to the pleasure I'm relishing in.

His dick thickens inside me, pulsing as he washes my insides with his cum. My heart is racing, my lungs burn as I gasp for my next breath. He leans forward, careful not to give any weight to my stomach as he connects our foreheads.

"I'll never get enough of you, and that sweet pussy clenching around me in all the right ways."

"Is there a wrong way for my pussy to clench?" I wonder out loud.

He barks out a laugh and makes his dick slip free of my pussy.

"Shit," he grunts and leans back, only to groan. "Daaamn. Now that's sexy. My cum leaking from your pink, puffy cunt. Lips spread, glistening… damn. I'm getting hard again. If you weren't pregnant, I'd keep you filled with my cum day in, day out."

I rub my overly present belly. I'm still trying to catch my breath so words aren't tumbling freely from my mouth. And really, what can I reply to his statement? As long as there are orgasms around, you'll never hear me complain? I'm pretty sure he knows where we stand on this 'cause sex is one of the many things we're always in agreement about.

I glance at the ring decorating my finger. The promise he gave me to make me his wife, the arrow symbolic to stand for the man behind the vow. The straight shooter, hitting my heart the second he entered my life.

For bad, for worse, for pleasure and beyond… he's there the way I'm here for him. Now and forever, we'll take the ride of our life shoulder to shoulder and heart to heart. Wherever it might lead us.

EPILOGUE

Three years later

ARROW

I throw some money on the counter for the bartender, and he stalks off as I take my beer.

"She looks like a handful," the fucker next to me says with glee as he jerks his chin in the direction of Ginny.

My old lady is sitting alone at a table across the room where I left her to get myself a drink. We're in a trucker's bar and there are only a handful of people sitting at the counter nursing their beer. It's late, I'm dead tired, and highly irritated with the fucker next to me who we have been following for three days straight.

"She is at times," I honestly agree. "But she knows how to submit."

There's a creepy glint in his eye when he says, "They all submit beautifully with the right motivation."

"That so?" I grunt, faking spiked interest as I take a sip of my beer. "Any hints and tips? Something to share? 'Cause that one there." I raise my beer in the direction of my old lady. "Is only playing the handful part 'cause she know I'll fuck her good." I take another swig of my drink and add in an afterthought loud enough for him to hear, "I hate it when the bitch fakes it. Makes me want to squeeze her throat slowly, letting her know her life is slipping away under my palm 'cause I'm the one in charge."

Staring at Ginny I let a genuine smile slide across my face.

Turning to the fucker next to me I tell him, "Maybe tonight I won't stop squeezing."

I place my empty glass on the counter and push away from the bar.

I'm about to walk away when the fucker grabs

my forearm. "Are you serious? Because if you are…I think we should talk some more."

Letting my gaze find Ginny, my partner in crime in all ways possible, I say, "I'm done talking."

I snap my fingers and point at the door. Ginny scrambles to her feet and rushes out the door.

The fucker chuckles. "You trained her well."

"Too well," I fake grumble, but the fucker laughs, thinking I'm serious. "Shame you don't have a woman so we could switch, it'll sure liven things up." Giving the fucker a nod, I tell him, "Nice talking to you. Enjoy the rest of your night."

I don't have to turn around to hear his footsteps following me out of the bar. Ginny is standing in the dimly lit parking lot, staring down at her feet near my bike. It's as if she's not paying attention to her surroundings, but she excels in undercover shit.

I hate putting her at risk and yet most of my fears concerning her safety are unwarranted. She definitely isn't the rookie cop I once met and asked for help when she was in a fucked-up situation herself. Nope.

She's highly trained with the experience of

working cases right along with me for the past three years. We work flawlessly together and it's why we were the only two people inside that bar tonight.

"Hold up," the fucker says and I come to a stop.

"Were you serious when you mentioned switching if I had a woman?" the fucker asks.

I keep referring to the man as "the fucker," inside my head, but I'm damn sure aware his name is Gael Patrick. Last witness to see not one, not two, but three women who went missing and turned up dead in a dumpster behind trucker bars like the one we just walked out of. All of them strangled, signs of being tied up and tortured for days.

"Dead serious," I tell him and let my tongue slide over my bottom lip, faking interest when I ask, "Why? Do you have something to offer me if I let you have a go at my woman?"

A shocked, "No. Please," comes from my woman.

Gael shoots me a grin. "Bring her and I'll show you."

I snap my fingers in Ginny's direction and she

instantly shakes her head. I mutter a curse under my breath and stomp her way. I raise my head and she flinches. My heart tugs, recognizing her move for what it is; a real emotion.

This case is close to heart when it comes to memories of what she experienced hints off. I'd never–fucking never for whatever case or need–reach out to grab her hair. Deep down she knows it, but you can't hide scars...even the mental ones who have had years to heal.

Fisting the fabric of the front of her shirt, I tug her along and she plays her part by dragging her feet and digging her nails into my wrist.

"Please, please, please," she starts to sob.

I know my woman, my old lady, my wife, the mother of my child through and through. Her voice when she uses that word with sarcasm, in demand when she talks to our daughter, and especially when I fuck her and she wants something only I can give her.

But this word she's repeating over and over is a line falling from her lips the way an actor is doing a scene in front of the camera. Except for the cameras Gael is oblivious of are meant for the government to bring that fucker to justice as he leads us to his delivery truck parked in the darkness of the back of this parking lot.

Gael takes his keys from his pocket and opens the back. Jumping inside he holds out his greedy fingers in Ginny's direction.

"Give her to me and I'll lift her up," he says as he stares at my woman's tits.

"You're not touching my property until you show me yours," I grunt and wrap my arm around Ginny's waist to hoist her up against me as I grab the latch and easily lift the both of us into the back of the truck.

Gael is oblivious to me putting Ginny behind me as he rushes to the back of the cargo room. I know for a fact my wife is already palming a gun. This because we're fairly certain Gael is about to fuck up and show us he has a woman bound and gagged since we can see feet with painted toenails half hidden by boxes.

I have my hand on my own gun when muffled

whimpers fill the air as Gael disappears behind the boxes. He reappears two breaths later with indeed a woman who is bound and gagged. There are dark bruises littering her body and she's completely naked.

"Let her go and step away from the woman," Ginny's harsh voice fills the space.

"What the fuck?" Gael growls and his hand reaches for the gun I noticed behind his back when I spotted him at the bar.

The sound of a bullet whizzes through the air and Gael's body jerks. There are voices coming from behind us as we step aside to let our brothers pass. I follow once Vachs and Wyatt are crouching down next to Gael.

Ginny is right next to me and hands me a knife to cut away the duct tape from the woman who is staring at us with a load of panic in her eyes. Ginny carefully removes the gag from her mouth.

"Is he dead? Please tell me he's dead," the woman pleads.

"No, ma'am," Ginny calmly tells her. "He took

a bullet to the shoulder. Once he's treated, he will disappear behind bars."

The woman starts to sob and ramble about not being able to escape. Ginny guides her out of the delivery truck and hands her over to the awaiting EMTs.

"Another one in the bag," Archer says with pride as he comes to a stop next to us. "Wyatt just mentioned he found a box with pictures of the other women we found dead. All in the same state as the one you saved, bound and shoved behind those boxes. His personal porn stash of trophies. This case kinda reminds me of a case we had way back with the delivery guy of the diner of Rack's sister. Remember? The one where the fucker kept his wife in the refrigerated truck." He shivers and turns his attention to Ginny. "Nice aim."

Ginny shrugs. "Are we done here? If so, I'll gladly head to the hotel to catch some sleep. I'm beat."

"We'll take it from here, but—"

"Yeah, yeah," I grunt as I cut my prez off. "You'll have the report on your desk by tomorrow afternoon."

Archer chuckles. "Good. And remember–"

"Yeah, yeah." This time it's coming from Ginny. "Hunter's birthday party is this weekend. Blue balloons. I already bought some and have them in Arrow's saddle bags."

"Thank fuck," Archer mutters.

Now it's our time to chuckle as I lead my woman toward my bike. This was a long couple of days, but with this ending? Being able to find a woman alive in the hands of a serial killer? Yeah, definitely worth the tired bones.

It's a good thing we work in teams so the rest of the brothers can take over to wrap things up while we leave for the hotel room. A few hours of sleep before we head back home. It's a fifteen-minute ride and just the feel of her front plastered to my back soothes the turmoil of what we just went through.

Most missions are low risk, but some people are dicks with scrambled eggs for brains and can definitely cause more harm than good. Meaning we never know the outcome of a mission until everything is said and done.

I'm completely beat once we step inside our hotel room and ask, "Did you want to take a shower first?"

She reaches for her overnight bag. "No, you go first. I'm going to call Bee real quick."

I lift my hand to cup her cheek and she instantly leans into my touch. My chest squeezes a flow of love right from my heart and into my veins. This woman truly is my life's blood.

Our lips meet and I murmur against her mouth, "Let me know if she's still awake or finally sleeping."

"Will do," she whispers and steals another kiss.

I stroll to the bathroom and shed my clothes as I hear Ginny call Bee. Our daughter is a bit of a fussy sleeper and either goes to sleep late or wakes up in the middle of the night to stay awake for at least two hours before crashing.

Handling my business, it takes me less than fifteen minutes to shower and towel dry and then I'm finally sliding under the covers. My head hits the pillow when Ginny disappears into the bathroom to take a shower.

I settle on my back and spread my legs as I release a deep sigh and swing my arm over my tired eyes. I could easily drift off but refuse to fall asleep before I'm able to take my woman into my arms.

My breathing slows as I listen to her humming in the bathroom as she gets ready for bed. It's a routine I've heard and seen day in, day out in the years we've spent together. I'm thankful to hear tonight didn't rip open some of the mental scars I know are still there from her past.

Some cases come close to reminding her of what happened to her and yet she always stays focused. Like tonight when she shot that fucker in the shoulder instead of putting a bullet right between the eyes.

He deserved to be put down for what he did to all those women and yet Ginny took him out to be able to bring him to justice. I'm damn proud of her mindset, the way she handles herself, and everything else she does.

The bed dips and I'm a bit caught by surprise when the sheet slides from the lower half of my body.

I try to stay as still as possible because moments like these are rare. My cock isn't such a stealthy fucker, though. It twitches as soon as her fingers slide up my leg.

A soft chuckle comes from her and I dare to peek a glance from under my arm. Her eyes are set on my cock as she palms my length and leans in. Tongue sliding between her lips to lick the head and tease the slit. Fuck.

I want to reach out to grab her hand with both hands and keep her rooted as I shove my hips off the bed to fill her mouth with my cock. Something that I'll never do. I'm damn lucky to have her lips sucking my length between them, taking me in her hot mouth.

It took her over a year to ask if she could try to play with me. Fuck. I never knew I'd missed blow jobs until that very day. With what Fabio put her through, and the trauma she endured, I never expected a blow job due to obvious triggers.

Yet, I'll always give my woman what she needs and who am I to stop her if she wants to try giving me a blow job? The first time she cuffed both my hands above my head to make sure she was in full control and I let her play.

The whole thing lasted only four damn minutes. Uh huh. Teenage boy shit when I blew my load after feeling her suck me into her mouth for the very first time. Sprayed fucking everywhere.

Her face, hair, my groin, belly, the bed…like a damn volcano erupting after being sleeping for decades. Made her laugh, though. Hurt my pride and dented my ego, but she fucking bloomed after that experience and has been growing bolder in her blow jobs ever since.

I spread my legs some more to give her the extra room she needs to take me deep, to the back of her throat and…fuuuuuuck. I feel her fucking tonsils welcome me back. How tired I was a moment ago… that's how fueled with energy I am now.

The arm falls away from my face and I stare right into my woman's lust-filled eyes. The sight alone– her lips stretched wide around my cock–is enough to make me blow. But then she pops it free from her mouth and lazily tugs my glistening cock.

"What do you want, baby?" she asks with desire and mirth tainting her voice.

"Felt your mouth, now I want your pussy wrapped around my cock, tits bouncing in my face as you rip the cum from my body," I bluntly tell her.

She grins and eagerly crawls up my body, lining the blunt head of my length right up with her entrance. I can only stare as her greedy pussy sucks me in and swallows me fucking whole. That is until the sight of swaying tits drags my attention away.

Never a dull moment when you have a woman as captivating as mine. Even after years of both living and working together, we're still as in love as the day we both fell for one another. If. Not. More.

My fingers dig into her hips, helping her bounce on and off my cock as I snatch a nipple–that's right in front of my face–between my teeth. She groans in delight as I nip and suck, giving her the bite of pain with the pleasure we both enjoy.

I never last long when my woman is in charge and I should pull out and switch our positions so I can fuck her from behind while finger-fucking her dark hole, but the pleasure on her face as she stares down at me is enough to keep me rooted in place.

In the end, positions and who is taking the lead doesn't matter one damn bit as the both of us dive off the orgasm cliff and jump right into the bliss we created together. Utter perfection and I make it world news as I bellow her name, making it bounce off the walls.

Fuck. I wrap my arms tightly around her and sag back down into the mattress. My cock softens somewhat inside her pussy as we both pant for our next breath. Our skin is coated with a sheen of sweat and I'm not caring one bit that our mixed juices are slipping down my balls.

All is right in the world when I'm sated, in bed, with my wife in my arms. Though, I do need to know one thing before I can sleep.

My woman knows me too well when she mutters, "Josie fell asleep at nine and was still sleeping when I called."

I chuckle. "Why is it she always sleeps through the night when she's with Bee and we're working?"

"Beats me," Ginny grumbles. "But somehow it's good to know so we can fully focus on the job…and each other."

I squeeze her fine ass in my hands, my cock sadly slipping from her pussy. "Damn right."

She yawns and snuggles her face into the crook of my neck.

"Love you." Her voice is a mere whisper and the soft snore filling my ears lets me know she's already drifted off.

Apparently, I'm not the only one who's completely drained. I place a kiss on the side of her head.

"My love is endless and deeper than any ocean known to mankind, darlin," I murmur, knowing she can't hear me and yet she doesn't have to.

Because she gets those words from me daily while it's my actions that show her how fucking much she means to me. One only knows their life is complete when you find the person who completes you. It's then you become aware of what you were missing all along.

And it feels damn good to be complete and whole as I close my eyes and let sleep take me with the weight of my woman draped over my body.

THANK YOU

Thank you for reading Arrow's story.
Gaining exposure as an independent author
relies mostly on word-of-mouth, so if you have the
time and inclination, please consider leaving a short
review wherever you can. Even a short message on
social media would be greatly appreciated.

If you would like to read all the stories of the
first and second generation of Broken Deeds MC?
Here's the link to all the books in this world:
https://books2read.com/rl/BrokenDeedsMC

SPECIAL THANKS

My beta team;
Lynne, Wendy, Neringa,
my pimp team,
and to you, as my reader…

Thanks so much!
You guys rock!

Contact:

I love hearing from my readers.

Email:

authoresthereschmidt@gmail.com

Or contact my PA **Christi Durbin**
for any questions you might have.
facebook.com/CMDurbin

Signup for Esther's newsletter:
esthereschmidt.nl/newsletter

Visit Esther E. Schmidt online:

Website:

www.esthereschmidt.nl

Facebook - AuthorEstherESchmidt

Twitter - @esthereschmidt

Instagram - @esthereschmidt

Pinterest - @esthereschmidt

Signup for Esther's newsletter:

esthereschmidt.nl/newsletter

Join Esther's fan group on Facebook:

www.facebook.com/groups/estherselite

MORE BOOKS

Printed in Great Britain
by Amazon